lucky

it girl novels created by Cecily von Ziegesar:

The It Girl
Notorious
Reckless
Unforgettable
Lucky

If you like **the it girl**, you may also enjoy:

Bass Ackwards and Belly Up by Elizabeth Craft and Sarah Fain
Secrets of My Hollywood Life by Jen Calonita
Haters by Alisa Valdes-Rodriguez

and keep your eye out for
Betwixt by Tara Bray Smith, coming October 2007

lucky

an it girl novel

CREATED BY

CECILY VON ZIEGESAR

poppy

LITTLE, BROWN AND COMPANY
New York   Boston

Little, Brown and Company

Poppy
Hachette Book Group
237 Park Avenue, New York, NY 10017
Visit our Web site at www.pickapoppy.com

First Edition: November 2007

ALLOYENTERTAINMENT   Produced by Alloy Entertainment
151 West 26th Street, New York, NY 10001

ISBN-13: 978-0-316-11347-2
ISBN-10: 0-316-11347-6

10 9 8 7 6 5 4 3 2 1
CWO
Printed in the United States of America

lucky

I've been lucky. I'll be lucky again.

—Bette Davis

A WAVERLY OWL ALWAYS TURNS
A DEAF EAR TO GOSSIP.

The crisp smell of autumn at Waverly Academy had been replaced by the undeniable scent of smoke—and not the pleasant, leaf-burning kind. It was an acrid, nose-hair-tingling burned-hay stench that reminded Jenny Humphrey that *someone* had set the barn at the Miller farm ablaze at last night's Cinephiles party. Maybe it was an accident. Or maybe not.

Jenny pushed open the dining hall's heavy wooden door and made her way across the cavernous room toward the food line. It was a long walk in plain view of every packed table, and Jenny tried to focus on the morning sun pouring through the stained glass windows rather than on the whispers that reverberated off the cathedral-like ceilings. Waverly Owls were notorious gossips, but there was even more to talk about today than usual.

She filled her tray with special Saturday morning apple-cinnamon pancakes and maneuvered her way through the long oak tables toward the corner, where she spotted Alison Quentin's head of glossy black hair. A small blond girl was wedged in between Alison and Sage Francis. Jenny checked to see that her roommate, Callie, and her ex, Easy, weren't seated at the same table. After catching Callie and Easy *together* in the barn last night, she never wanted to see either of them again. If she hadn't shared that unexpected, unbelievably sweet kiss with Julian McCafferty right afterward, she might have skipped out on breakfast/Waverly/life altogether. Her stomach fluttered just thinking about it.

"New meat," came a voice from behind Jenny. She turned to see Celine Colista, the olive-skinned cocaptain of the field hockey team, gesturing toward the small blond girl sitting between Alison and Sage. She watered down some fresh-squeezed OJ and placed it on her tray. "They're around all week."

"New meat?"

"Prospective students," Celine explained impatiently as they approached the table together. "We're not supposed to say pre-fresh*men* because it's, you know, sexist and all." Jenny and Celine set their trays down next to Alison.

Jenny leaned forward and smiled at the blond pre-frosh. The girl was even tinier up close. "Hi. I'm Jenny."

"I'm Chloe." The girl pushed up her black rectangular-framed Ralph Lauren glasses and nodded in Jenny's direction.

"She's following Alison around," Benny Cunningham announced loudly, leaning her elbows on the dark wooden table.

She pushed her long, stick-straight brown hair away from her horsey but pretty face. "Where you from again, new meat?"

"Putney," Chloe answered timidly. She picked an invisible piece of lint off her pale blue J.Crew cable-knit sweater. "It's in Vermont."

With her pale skin and wide innocent blue eyes, Chloe looked like Dakota Fanning. It was hard for Jenny to imagine being mean to Dakota Fanning. "Vermont is really pretty," she offered, hoping to make the younger girl feel more comfortable. Jenny knew what it felt like to be the awkward new girl at Waverly. She cringed, remembering how clueless Old Jenny had been when she first arrived several weeks ago. But New Jenny sat at the coolest table in the dining hall, went to crazy parties in burning barns, and kissed adorable boys under the moonlight. Take that, Old Jenny.

Suddenly a cheer echoed off the high, sloping ceilings of the dining hall, and Jenny turned to see Heath Ferro standing at a nearby table, his arms thrown up in triumph. Sunlight glinted off his artfully tousled dirty-blond hair, and cracker crumbs spewed out of his mouth. He'd obviously just completed the saltine challenge, a feat much attempted in the Waverly dining hall: downing six of the super-dry crackers in less than a minute without drinking any water. Heath collected high fives from a group of guys gathered around him, including some prepubescent ones. Jenny noticed then that there were at least a dozen prospectives scattered at various tables, all staying close to their assigned Owls, like city tourists too afraid to stray more than a few paces from their guides.

"So, did you hear the latest?" Sage leaned forward in her chair, her aqua blue eyes shining. She pulled up the sleeves of her Elie Tahari midnight blue tunic sweater, as if spreading gossip would entail getting her hands dirty.

"What?" Jenny asked as she forked a piece of pancake and swished it through a puddle of pure New England maple syrup. She wore her favorite Earl jeans and a black turtleneck from the Gap that she'd had since eighth grade. She was underdressed compared to Sage and Benny, but that was only because girls at Waverly used almost any activity as an excuse for a fashion show.

"They found a lighter in the barn." Benny grinned mischievously. Her white teeth matched her white Vince double-gauze tee, making her look like an advertisement for Crest White-strips. Though given her multimillion-dollar trust fund, it was probably due to professional whitening. "It had a student's initials on it. Julian McCafferty's."

Jenny put the forkful of pancake down on her plate. *Julian?*

"I heard it was some guys from St. Lucius," Celine said in a half whisper, leaning forward and tucking a lock of black hair behind her ear. "But I also heard it was that skeezy Dan guy, Heath's liquor store connection?" She ran her tongue across her front teeth, finally dislodging the spinach from her omelet that had been stuck there the whole meal. "Oh, and Simone said it was some townie pyro who didn't get into Waverly."

"Juicy," Alison chimed in. She took a sip of her orange juice, seemingly unfazed by the idea that there might be a jealous Rhinecliff local lashing out at Waverly students.

"I heard there were some people *smoking* in the barn," Chloe piped up helpfully. She stabbed at a slice of French toast.

"Where did you hear that?" Jenny managed to ask. Last night, she'd confronted Callie about the fact that she and Easy had been smoking in the barn right before it went up in flames, but she wasn't sure anyone else knew. Callie had retorted that *Jenny* probably set the barn on fire out of jealousy. She knew Callie was just being defensive and melodramatic, but she was still angry about it. If the rest of Waverly found out that Callie and Easy had been smoking in the barn—well, Jenny wasn't going to stop *that* rumor from spreading. She honestly wouldn't be sorry to see them go. It would serve them right for being such . . . horny *jerks*.

"Yeah. And *who* was smoking?" Benny demanded, looking at Chloe with interest for the first time. "You've only been here like an hour. How would you even know?"

"I just heard it." Chloe shrugged, seemingly unfazed by the elder girl's aggressive stare. "I can't remember where." She looked around the dining hall and then added, "Is there powdered sugar anywhere?"

Jenny didn't know why she'd been worried about Chloe. She was going to be fine.

"I heard it was Easy and Callie," Sage offered quietly, pushing her tray of half-eaten food toward the center of the table. She pulled her flaxen hair back into a loose ponytail. "We all saw them coming from the barn . . . and you know they both smoke." She shrugged, leaving everyone else to put the pieces together.

"Who smokes?" Ryan Reynolds demanded as he crashed his heavily laden tray down on their table, his full Coke glass sloshing onto his plate of food. Jenny recoiled. Soda at breakfast? Gross. He scooted the chair closer to Sage and perched his head on his hand, waiting for her to continue.

"Uh, me." Sage's pale cheeks turned pink. "And, like, half the campus."

"Tell me something I don't know." Ryan tried to grab a piece of Sage's long, butter-blond hair, but she squealed and squirmed out of his reach. "Has anybody seen Callie this morning?" he asked. Jenny looked at Ryan curiously, trying to figure out what was different about him this morning. He looked . . . more responsible, somehow, which was the last word that usually came to mind when describing Ryan Reynolds. She quickly realized it was because she'd never seen him wear glasses before. Given that his dad invented soft contact lenses, he was probably never in short supply of those. "I need to copy her Latin homework."

"Stables," Benny replied instantly, shoveling a mouthful of bacon. "With Eaaasssssyyyyy."

"What would they be doing in a stable?" Chloe asked innocently.

Benny and Celine laughed knowingly. "Rolling and jumping in the hay!" Celine snorted gleefully. She took off her Waverly field hockey zip-up sweatshirt, revealing a tight black T-shirt underneath, and Ryan immediately stole a sideways glance at her chest.

"Let's hope they don't set it on fire, too." Sage laughed.

Chloe looked perplexed but didn't say anything, lowering her eyes to her French toast instead.

Jenny stood up from the table and mumbled something about an upset stomach, her fluffy pancakes practically untouched. She grabbed her cell and headed for the door.

Five minutes later, she stood on the gray stone steps of the dining hall, waiting for Julian. As soon as she'd gotten up from the table she'd texted him, asking him to meet her. If he was in trouble, she needed to warn him right away.

And of course, she didn't exactly mind having an excuse to see him again.

Rumors about the fire swirled around her head. Could Dan the Liquor Man really have had anything to do with it, besides supplying a bunch of rowdy kids with booze? Was it possible some crazy townie hated Waverly kids enough to try to set them on fire? And what was Julian's lighter doing in the barn? He'd lost it, hadn't he? She thought she remembered him saying something about losing it . . . and he couldn't really have started the fire, because he'd been with *her*, kissing her so sweetly outside the barn and making her forget all about Easy and Callie and what she'd just seen. Another thought occurred to Jenny then: *Could* Easy and Callie have started it? She pictured them lying together in the hay, laughing and smoking and being careless as ever. They might have been careless about *her* feelings, but surely they weren't arsonists. Just liars. She shook her head, her brunette curls swinging like thick vines. No matter how hard she tried to shake the thought away, Jenny kept coming to the same conclusion: She was just a blip on Easy's radar, a distraction in between breaking up with Callie and getting back together with her.

"Hi."

She spun around to see Julian's grinning face. He tugged the zipper of his faded gray Everlast hoodie up to his chin.

"Hey," Jenny replied, a wave of pleasure washing over her at the sight of the tall, shaggy-haired freshman. She took a step toward him and craned her neck to look into his warm brown eyes. She wanted to kick herself for wearing her flat navy Keds with the little butterflies on them. If she was going to spend more time with Julian in the future, she'd need to wear her tallest Michael Kors wedges.

"Did you eat already?" He hopped off the last step and landed with a thud in front of her. His shaggy brown-blond hair fluttered around his face. He looked like a golden retriever who'd found his tennis ball. But in a hot-boy sort of way.

"Yeah," Jenny lied. After hearing all those rumors, eating had been out of the question. Even now, her stomach was still doing somersaults—but in a different way now.

"Wanna go up Hopkins Hill?" Julian asked, nodding toward the bluffs behind her. She wondered if he was thinking about their kiss last night, too. He *had* to be thinking about it, right?

"Let's go," she replied gamely.

They started up the path through the woods to the bluffs. The crash of plates in the dining hall kitchen was slowly replaced by the chirping of birds and the soft, wind-in-the-forest sounds

Jenny was still getting used to after spending her entire life in New York City. The soles of their sneakers padded against the dry leaves on the path.

They reached a small clearing, and Julian came to a stop. His soft brown eyes landed on her lips, and Jenny blushed. Was he going to kiss her again? she wondered. "Did you and Callie talk?"

Jenny felt her face grow hot at the memory of confronting Callie last night. She'd been furious—not that Callie and Easy were together again, but that Callie had lied to her about it and pretended they were all buddy-buddy. Really, she and Easy were probably laughing at her while they snuggled naked in the barn and smoked cigarettes and set the whole place on fire. "Yeah, sort of. I mean, I don't really know."

"It's cool." Julian crouched down, plucked a brilliant red oak leaf from the path, and held it out to Jenny as if it were a flower. She giggled and took the leaf from him, letting her hand brush against his. "You don't have to go into it. I just wondered if you guys figured it out." He shrugged his sloping shoulders gently and Jenny noticed he was wearing a very familiar outfit: black Tretorns, dark-wash True Religion jeans with fist-size holes in the knees, and a black T-shirt underneath his hoodie.

"Have you been up all night?" she asked.

He rubbed his hand against the back of his neck, kicking his toes against the dirt path. "Do I smell?" He lowered his voice a little, as if someone might overhear.

"No." She giggled. He actually smelled kind of nice, like

pine trees. Or maybe it was just because they were in the woods. "But you're wearing the same clothes as last night."

"Yeah, I actually walked home." Julian hitched up the sagging waist of his jeans. His boxers were light green with tiny white sheep printed on them. Jenny blushed at the sight of them. "There's a shortcut through the gulley behind the Miller farm," he explained.

"Oh," she said simply, as if that explained it. Walking around all night by yourself? Boys were so weird. When she'd been with Easy, he'd painted in his special spot deep in the woods. And back home, whenever she'd walk through Sheep Meadow, it was littered with boys smoking joints and communing with the closest thing to nature New York could provide. Or maybe they just wanted to get buzzed. Jenny leaned against a mossy tree trunk, trying to act casual under Julian's steady gaze. She didn't care if she was getting her clothes a little dirty. He was worth it.

His eyes traced her lips. "The whole sky was lit red and white and blue from the lights on the police cars and fire trucks," he added. "It was actually sort of cool." Jenny smiled at his boyish enthusiasm. She loved the idea of him taking off on a whim, making his way through the woods in the dead of night, replaying their kiss in his mind as he walked.

"Julian," she began, "have you seen your lighter recently?"

A strange look crossed his face. She could tell he'd already heard it had been found.

"You can just tell Dean Marymount you lost it," she went on. When she first saw him that night in Dumbarton—hiding in the broom closet—he'd been looking for his Zippo. At least, that's what he'd said. "If you tell them the truth, there's no way you'll get kicked out."

Julian just shrugged and stared at something over Jenny's head. She hoped a tarantula wasn't crawling down the tree, about to make a nest in her curls. "I'm not too worried," he finally answered. He took a step closer to Jenny, planting his hands against the tree trunk on either side of her so that she was trapped. Not that she minded. "I've got the cutest alibi on campus." A grin curled the sides of his mouth.

Jenny immediately lost her train of thought, distracted again by the memory of their lips pressed together, alone in the dark. And a moment later, it was more than just a memory.

OwlNet

From: DeanMarymount@waverly.edu
To: Waverly Academy
Date: Saturday, October 12, 10:15 A.M.
Subject: Prospective Students

Dear Students, Faculty, and Staff,

As you're probably aware, we have a number of prospective students visiting our campus this weekend. These visits are an important chance for prospective students to get a taste for Waverly Academy, and I trust everyone has been making the prospectives feel welcome. Thank you to all those Owls who have graciously taken on the role of host. Prospectives will be on campus until Wednesday in order to sit in on two full days of classes, so please continue your hospitality for the duration of their stay.

A special formal dinner will take place Monday night in the dining hall in honor of the prospective students. Dress according to code.

I also trust that the behavior of students over the next few days will be more restrained than it has been in the past few weeks.

Best,

Dean Marymount

RyanReynolds: You and Kara, huh? So that's why we've never hooked up!

BrettMesserschmidt: No. That would be because I hate you. ☺

RyanReynolds: Oh.

From: JeremiahMortimer@stlucius.edu
To: BrettMesserschmidt@waverly.edu
Date: Saturday, October 12, 11:08 A.M.
Subject: You okay?

Hey,

I know you're still not talking to me, but I heard about the fire at the Miller farm and I wanted to make sure you were okay. I heard some other stuff, too, but don't worry, I don't believe a word of it—I know you. And I know you're probably pretty upset that there are people talking about you or whatever. Let me know if you want to talk or anything.

Anyway, hope you're well.

—J.

AlisonQuentin: Hey sexy. Whatcha up to?

AlanStGirard: Think I'll stay in bed all day. Too much drama for me.

AlisonQuentin: You hear about Julian's Zippo? He doesn't act like a pyro.

AlanStGirard: Yeah, but I also heard Tinsley was hanging around the barn.

AlisonQuentin: Thought guys liked girls w/ a wild side?

AlanStGirard: Wild yes, pyro no.

AlisonQuentin: In that case, meet me at the gazebo this afternoon. I'll show you wild.

AlanStGirard: For that, I'll get out of bed. Or maybe you'd like to join me?

A WAVERLY OWL NEVER DOUBTS HER CHOSEN
COURSE OF ACTION.

Brett Messerschmidt stared at the cover of her Latin text-book, the old Flaming Lips song "She Don't Use Jelly" blasting from her iPod dock. The Doric columns on the cover stared back at her, and she wished she could close her eyes and transport herself back in time. Ancient Rome. The 1920s. Woodstock. Pompeii. Anywhere but Waverly Academy, circa now.

If only Heath had been the one responsible for spilling the beans about her and Kara to the whole world, she could've been angry instead of upset. She wanted to take it out on someone, anyone. Anyone but Kara, even though it was, technically, all Kara's fault for telling Callie they'd been hooking up in secret. She toyed with the idea of being mad at Callie for being a light-weight with a penchant for drunken gossip, but that didn't exactly satisfy her, either.

She leaned back in her uncomfortable wooden desk chair, pressing her vertebrae against the hard wooden slats. She really liked Kara, but were they, like, a *couple* now? Would that make them Waverly's token lesbian couple? She envisioned a Waverly tour guide leading a flock of prospective students and their parents around campus and pointing at Brett's window. "Welcome to Dumbarton, proud home of Waverly's only lesbians!"

She let her forehead rest against the cool surface of her desk, her hands gripping the short red pigtails she'd put her hair into that morning. She felt like Pippi Longstocking, except Pippi probably didn't kiss girls. At least Tinsley had the decency to be gone. Brett had dragged her exhausted body out of bed this morning to be greeted by a pleasantly empty room, only a trace of Tinsley's Yves St. Laurent Baby Doll hanging in the air.

"Hello?" Kara Whalen's face peeked through the doorway. A pair of tortoiseshell cat-eye glasses magnified her wide hazel eyes as they nervously scanned the room. Her light brown hair just grazed her shoulders. "Tinsley around?"

"She's out." Brett sat up in her chair and twisted a pigtail around her finger.

Kara looked relieved. "I thought I heard her out on the quad." She sat gingerly down on Brett's bed, wearing a fitted gray NYU T-shirt that hugged her curves, and a pair of faded jeans.

"I've never seen you wear glasses before." Brett pushed her Latin textbook away from her and turned toward Kara. "Very sexy-librarian." She felt her face flush. Did she have to say *sexy*?

"Thanks." Kara grinned and straightened the red bobby pin

that was holding a lock of her silky brown hair away from her face. It reminded Brett of when she was little and used paper clips to hold back her dolls' hair. "All the smoke made my eyes sting. I couldn't get my contacts in this morning."

Brett nodded. She didn't want to think about last night anymore. She'd spent her first two years at Waverly afraid that everyone would find out she was the daughter of a plastic surgeon and grew up in a tacky McMansion in Jersey. Now her gold-plated, leopard-print past didn't even seem like a big deal anymore. She smoothed out the wrinkles in her white Theory peasant shirt. There had been a fire. She had a *girl*friend. Her past was the least of her worries.

"I didn't see you at breakfast." Kara picked up a copy of *Absinthe*, Waverly's art magazine, from Brett's night table and flipped through the pages. Brett rarely ever read the magazine, but it was delivered in all of the students' mailboxes, and she sort of liked to keep it around. She thought maybe it made her seem edgy, in a good way. But given recent events, she'd probably never need to convince anyone she was edgy again. Kara peeked at Brett over the top of her glasses.

Brett stood up and stretched. Her bare toes dug into the soft, mint green chenille rug. She'd purposely skipped breakfast, hoping to avoid all the rumors swirling in the dining hall. She was sort of amazed that Kara had wandered right into the lion's den. "Did I miss anything?"

"Apple-cinnamon pancakes." Kara studied the art section, flipping through the portfolio of abstract paintings. She smiled weakly at Brett.

"Did you find out anything more about the fire?" Brett asked. She was still standing in the middle of the room and wasn't sure whether or not to sit down on the bed next to Kara. She would've sat down on Tinsley's bed, except for the fact that (a) Tinsley was a raging bitch and (b) it was awkwardly far away. As soon as they'd been assigned to Dumbarton 121, Tinsley and Brett had pushed their beds to opposite ends of the room. She'd even considered hanging her baby blue seersucker-print Frette sheets from the ceiling to further divide the space.

"It's all everyone is talking about." Kara dropped the magazine on the bed and crossed her legs daintily. "People won't shut up about Easy and Callie. Oh, and they found a lighter in the remains, with that guy Julian McCafferty's initials on it. And some people think it was Tinsley who started it. Or the liquor store owner. I don't know. It could have been anyone."

Brett finally pushed the magazine out of the way and sat down on the silky fuchsia Indian-print comforter. A blue-and-white etching of a sailboat hung on the wall above them. Tinsley's grandfather had sent it, and Brett had rescued it from the garbage. Of course, Tinsley hadn't even bothered to open more than a corner of the package before tossing it.

Kara leaned in a little closer, and Brett could feel her warm breath tickle her skin. "I heard someone say they saw some boys from St. Lucius near the barn."

"Really?" A chill ran through Brett at the mention of St. Lucius, and she sat up a little straighter. Jeremiah had e-mailed her this morning, telling her he'd heard about the fire . . . and that he'd heard "some other things." What would he say if he found out that the rumors about her and Kara were true? And what was she possibly going to say in reply? She glanced over at her open iBook, as if it might hold the answer. She decided to wait to write back until she'd figured out what exactly was going on with Kara.

"What's the matter?" Kara demanded. She stared at Brett, and Brett looked away, focusing on the piles of yellow and orange leaves on the quad outside her window. "Hey." Kara placed her hand on Brett's ankle. "It's me. Remember?"

Brett felt herself soften under Kara's touch. She leaned her head closer to Kara's. They sat without saying anything for a while, and Brett again found herself drawn to the leaves outside. A yellow Frisbee flew into view. Benny Cunningham ran across the quad after it, laughing.

"I have an idea." Kara's hazel eyes perked up behind her glasses. "Forget this whole fire mess. How about we get into our pj's and go watch movies in the common room? I'm in the mood for something totally cheesy and ridiculous . . . like *Girls Just Wanna Have Fun.* It's so eighties, I love it." Kara eyed Brett hopefully.

Brett nodded noncommittally, tracing a finger over the fuchsia paisley print on her comforter. Watching cheesy movies with Kara sounded like the perfect thing to do. Except . . . in the Dumbarton common room? In their pj's? Wouldn't everyone assume they'd just, like, spent the night together? She found a loose thread in the fabric of the comforter and pulled it a little, watching as the fabric bunched up around it. Would

Kara be totally offended if she suggested hanging out in private instead?

Before she could say anything, the door swung open, knocking against the Degas print of ballet dancers on the wall behind it. Tinsley blew into the room, looking innocent in a baby blue oxford shirt and white eyelet skirt. Brett knew her roommate had dressed for calculated effect, because if there was anything Tinsley Carmichael *wasn't*, it was innocent.

"Hope I'm not disrupting anything, girls—or should I say girl*friends*?" she sneered cattily. Her dark ponytail bobbed as she opened and closed her desk drawer, quickly pocketing something that Brett couldn't see. She was gone again before Brett could even think of a nasty comeback to lob at her. The door slammed shut with a sound like a gunshot.

"Let's go." Kara stood, seemingly unfazed by Tinsley's catty jeer. *"Girlfriend,"* she added with a teasing grin. She must have seen the dismayed look on Brett's face, because her hazel eyes filled with concern. "Oh come on, are you really going to let *her* get to you?" She emphasized the word *her*, as if Tinsley were some sort of disagreeable pest that had yet to be exterminated.

"No . . ." Brett shook her head slowly, then more definitively. Tinsley was just being her usual bitchy self. But the problem was, it wasn't just Tinsley who was getting to her. It was the whispers at the party last night, the e-mail from Jeremiah, the jittery feeling in her stomach.

"She's just trying to get under your skin. And don't worry." Kara approached the doorway and turned to face Brett. She shoved her hands in the pockets of her jeans. "We don't have to use that title if you don't want to."

"Oh," Brett said automatically, before she could think of anything else to say. "Um, okay."

Kara shrugged easily, and Brett envied her composure. "No need for things to get all dramatic. We're seventeen—we don't even know what we're doing," she said matter-of-factly. "Anyway, should we go see if anything's on TV before we leave to get a movie?" She tilted her head in the direction of the common room, the relationship portion of the conversation now apparently over. Brett loved the way Kara could transition so easily from heavy subjects to light. She made everything seem so simple.

Brett stood and pulled down on the waistband of her black J.Crew drawstring pants, which had ridden up. "Maybe we should just hang out in your room instead," she suggested. "We could play Boggle. I'm an ace at Boggle," she added with a small smile. She felt a thousand times more relaxed at the thought of being alone. Kara had a single down the hall, which meant they could hang out in peace, without sneering roommates or nosy Dumbarton girls.

Kara shrugged her shoulders. "Sure," she agreed, leading the way out.

Brett followed, smiling. Kara was so easy to be with. And they were lucky she had a single. Living in a dorm with three hundred gossip-hungry girls wasn't exactly conducive to privacy. But so long as they were able to keep a low profile, this could end up being the best relationship she'd ever been in.

A WAVERLY OWL RESPECTS HER ELDERS—
ESPECIALLY WHEN SHE'S MANIPULATING THEM.

Tinsley Carmichael stood in the waiting area outside
Dean Marymount's office, eyeing Mr. Tomkins's desk.
She'd never seen it deserted before. The prematurely
bald administrative assistant was like a guard dog—always
there, and extremely, almost stupidly loyal. Tinsley opened the
top drawer of the dark oak desk, which was empty except for an
open pack of spearmint chewing gum, a Sacagawea gold dollar,
and a silver Tiffany charm bracelet with only one charm, a tiny
teapot. Weird. Tinsley unsheathed a stick of gum and popped it
into her mouth, wondering what else of interest there might be
in the room. The space looked as though it had been decorated
with pieces from the *Masterpiece Theatre* collection, with its
heavy oak paneling and tall bookshelves filled with green, red,
and black books with gold lettering. She could only imagine
how intimidated other students must have felt standing at the

gateway to Marymount's office. She herself had stood here many times before. But today, her mission was graver than ever.

After seeing Jenny and Julian kiss last night, she'd been too furious to sleep. She'd stayed up most of the night, staring out at the Hudson River through her window, feeling stupid for falling for Julian in the first place. As the sky started to lighten, she fantasized about building a little raft out of branches and twigs or whatever and floating down the river to Manhattan, where people were probably still awake, and where there were guys even hotter than Julian, who was only a freshman anyway. It would serve everyone right if she mysteriously disappeared. What would they do without her?

But fantasizing about leaving was the stuff of late-night desperation. Today was a new day. She took out her phone and tapped at the buttons with her unpolished, nicely buffed nails.

"Hello?" Callie's voice sounded far away.

"Where are you? We're supposed to be meeting now." Tinsley kept her voice down so Dean Marymount wouldn't hear. His assistant might be out enjoying the weekend, but Marymount was a workaholic, so she knew she'd find him in his office on a Saturday—especially given last night's events.

"Oh, right." Callie's voice was lazy and slow, as if she had just woken up from a nap. "I'm with Easy. Is it okay if we do it later?"

She heard Easy murmur something in the background, and then Callie giggled.

Tinsley rolled her violet eyes. "But I'm here *now*. Are you even listening?" She tried to keep the impatience out of her voice. Outside the enormous bay window a heavy, rain-bloated cloud passed overhead, and a few tiny sprinkles of rain scattered on the windowpane. She hoped Easy and Callie were out in the open somewhere so that they'd be forced to get the hell off each other.

"Yes, I'm listening." Whisper, whisper, shuffle. Giggle. "I just can't meet up with you right now. *Stop* it."

Tinsley checked her silver Movado watch impatiently. "Stop what?"

"I was talking to Easy," Callie explained with another stupid giggle. "I said *stop* it!" she shrieked.

"Are you going to help me out or what?" Tinsley demanded angrily, forgetting to whisper. She wished she had her Blue-tooth with her, but she hadn't had time to grab it from her room, not wanting to linger and make small talk with Brett and her lesbian lover.

"Yes. I said yes, okay?" Callie snapped in a hushed whisper, as if she didn't want Easy to overhear. "I just can't come right now. You can go ahead and do it without me. You'll probably be better off on your own anyway."

"Fine." Tinsley turned off her phone and shoved it into her tan suede Calypso purse. As annoying as it was to have Callie bail on her, she was right—she probably would be better alone. She took a deep breath before taking a step toward the walnut door of the dean's office.

"Come in!" he bellowed in response to Tinsley's hesitant knock. Dean Marymount didn't look up when she entered. His sandy comb-over fell loose as he bent over his desk, examining the sheet of paper in his hand. Wearing a bright yellow argyle sweater vest, he looked like Mr. Rogers's evil twin: utterly suburban, yet somehow menacing.

"Dean Marymount?" Tinsley used her best little-girl voice. Her straight dark hair was pulled back into a neat ponytail at the nape of her neck, and her face appeared makeupless and innocent—or at least, that was the idea. Of course, she had thrown Julian's lighter on the ground outside the barn after seeing him with Jenny, which had started the infamous fire. And that made her decidedly less than innocent. Unless she convinced Dean Marymount otherwise, her ass was toast. Even if it *was* the most perfect ass at Waverly. "Don't you ever take a day off?"

Marymount patted down his scraggly hair and sighed wearily. "Governing this student body is a full-time job, Ms. Carmichael." He gave her a long, disapproving stare. His normally organized desk was a mess of files and papers. Behind him, the enormous, second-floor bay windows gave way to an expansive view of Waverly's campus. She briefly wondered if the dean had purposely designed it that way, so he could watch his students like a hawk from dawn till dusk. She pictured him swooping down and snatching up an unsuspecting student with his angry talons, before pecking away at his flesh with his carnivorous beak.

"I've met some of the prospectives," Tinsley lied, trying to shake the image of her dean as a raptor-like bird. Plus, a little small talk might help her cause. She shuffled her feet nervously. "They seem like good Owls."

"Wonderful timing, isn't it?" Marymount complained,

throwing his Cross pen down on his oversize leather-framed desk calendar and running a hand through his thinning hair. "How do you think it looks to have arsonists on the loose?"

Tinsley knew the question was rhetorical, but it gave her the opening she was looking for. "That's why I've come to see you, sir." She took a small step forward onto the plush Turkish carpet, trying to erase the memory of when she'd last stood in this exact spot. Just a few days ago, she'd pressured the long-married dean to approve the off-campus Cinephiles barn party, using the fact that he was having an affair with the also-very-married dorm adviser Angelica Pardee as leverage against him. He'd agreed to the party but had told her that he'd hold her responsible for anything that went wrong. And things had definitely gone wrong. They couldn't get any more wrong. But if Tinsley had her way, she'd set them straight again. And she *always* got her way.

Marymount pushed back from his desk and laced his fingers across his stomach. The antique clock perched on one of the bookshelves in the corner chimed piercingly. "I needn't remind you of our last meeting, Ms. Carmichael."

Tinsley shook her head quickly. She knew he didn't expect an answer, and she wasn't going to give him the nervous mumble he was looking for. Instead, she fixed her gaze on the silver picture frame that sat on his desk. The family photo was now angled outward, as if Marymount couldn't bear to have his wife's picture staring him in the face all day long. The photograph must have included his extended family, because she noticed now that a dozen or so people were crowded into the frame. She singled out what must have been his niece, since the dean's children were already in college. The girl's hair was parted down the middle and she was wearing pink overalls. Her black glasses encircled a pair of frightened-looking blue eyes. The girl was in serious need of a makeover.

Dean Marymount picked up his pen and held it, as if ready to sign Tinsley's expulsion letter at a moment's notice. "And I suppose you've come because you know who started the fire?"

Tinsley looked down at the toes of her Miu Miu mary-janes. A mistake, she realized, as soon as she did. If you looked at your shoes, people assumed you were lying. The only thing worse was scratching your nose—everyone knew that. The trick was to look them straight in the eyes—or between their eyes. She focused on the tusky gray-brown hairs between Marymount's eyebrows. "Not exactly. But I know who *didn't* do it."

A thin smile broke out on Marymount's lips, as if he was willing to allow himself this minor amusement. "Who *didn't* do it?"

"Well, I heard you found Julian McCafferty's Zippo, but I know for a fact he gave that lighter to *Jenny Humphrey,*" Tinsley pressed on, continuing to stare at his eyebrow hairs in case she lost her nerve. They looked like sandy gray buds forcing their way through his forehead. Maybe they'd blossom in spring.

"I haven't interrogated Mr. McCafferty yet." Marymount picked up the paper and examined it, his sharp blue eyes running over lines of print. Tinsley took a step closer to his desk.

He flicked a finger against the paper. "This is the police report from the fire. It says the fire was without doubt started by an incendiary device."

"Jenny was in the barn before it caught fire," Tinsley insisted. One of the trees outside the window swayed in the breeze, and she was momentarily blinded by a sharp glint of sunlight. She squinted, hoping the dean didn't mistake the movement for a flinch. She knew that one wrong move could mean the difference between Jenny's expulsion and her own.

"What's all this about blaming Jennifer Humphrey?" Marymount picked up a heavy brass paperweight in the shape of an owl and turned it over in his hand. He peered at her over the gold rims of his glasses with his piercing blue eyes. "Did you two have a fight?"

Tinsley felt her shoulders tense up. A fight? Not exactly. It was more like a long, drawn-out war, started when Jenny appeared with her enormous chest and decided she could just throw herself at any guy on campus regardless of who he happened to be with at the time. "If you're worried that I have an ulterior motive, then just ask Callie Vernon. She was in the barn. She saw Jenny, too." Tinsley crossed her arms over her chest. It was about time Callie got off of Easy and pulled her weight.

"What was *Ms. Vernon* doing in the barn?" The dean leaned forward. She hadn't realized how suspicious her explanation might sound. Oops. Marymount's e-mail alert dinged. His eyes flicked to his flat-screen monitor for a moment and then settled back on Tinsley.

"She was with Easy Walsh . . . um . . . talking. He saw Jenny, too," she added hastily. If she wasn't careful, she'd tell him *she* started the fire. Shit. What was wrong with her?

Marymount gave a little snort of laughter. "Our list of possible suspects is growing exponentially by the minute," he declared, looking almost gleeful.

Tinsley suddenly noticed that the Trident spearmint gum in her mouth had lost all its flavor. "They didn't have anything to do with the fire," she insisted. She perched her hands firmly on her slim hips, desperate to not *seem* desperate. "But they saw Jenny. She started it. I'm positive it was her."

Marymount pushed his chair back and stood up, indicating that their meeting was nearing its conclusion. "You don't mind if I don't take your word for that, do you?" Another rhetorical question. Tinsley blinked her violet-colored eyes at him. "I appreciate your taking time from your Saturday morning to drop in." He shuffled the papers on his desk and then placed the police report in his top drawer, closing it with an ominous thud and locking it, pocketing the key. "I'll overlook your careless-ness in organizing the disastrous event, for now. But I'm sure we'll talk soon."

Tinsley turned and walked out into the empty outer office, closing Dean Marymount's door behind her. She stood in front of Mr. Tomkins's empty desk. She lunged forward and grabbed another piece of gum from the top drawer, sticking the old piece underneath the desk. Childish, yes, but she was pissed, and not about to restrain herself. She wasn't used to not get-ting her way. And she would stop at nothing to see that in this case—the case of Jenny Humphrey getting booted out of Waverly on her big-boobed ass—that she got *exactly* what she wanted *and* deserved. After all, she'd always been lucky, and this fire incident would be no exception. She and her friends would stay, and Jenny Humphrey would go.

A SMART OWL KNOWS THAT THE WAVERLY STABLES ARE INTENDED FOR RECREATIONAL PURPOSES.

Callie Vernon reluctantly pushed Easy Walsh's bare arm away from her and sat up, grabbing her new Stella McCartney jeans from the rumpled pile on the stable floor where all of their clothes had ended up an hour ago. They were in a section of the Waverly riding stables that no longer held horses, where no one ever came. Of course, though the horses were no longer around, their smell lingered. But it was better than the oppressive smell of smoke that hung like a cloak over the campus.

"No, not yet . . ." Easy pulled at the legs of the jeans to keep Callie from tugging them on. She giggled and danced out of his reach. The brown canvas horse blanket they'd been lying on—it was clean, Easy had promised—was scratchy beneath her bare feet, although she hadn't even noticed when it was touching the rest of her naked skin. Her mind, apparently, had been elsewhere.

She stared down at Easy's bare chest, at the birthmark below his rib cage, at the waistband of his charcoal gray Calvin Klein boxers. His body was always toned, despite the fact that he never went to the gym, and he always had defined ab muscles from riding his horse, Credo. He was so effortlessly *gorgeous*. And once more, he was all hers, every delicious inch of him.

"We should really get a nicer blanket out here." She stuck her bare, skinny arms through the spaghetti straps of her pale pink Cosabella camisole and shook her wavy strawberry blond hair out of her eyes.

"What, stiff canvas doesn't turn you on?" Easy drawled in his slight Kentucky accent. He grabbed Callie's folded cream-colored Ralph Lauren peacoat off the stable floor, wedging it under his head like a pillow with an easy grin. She knelt down and tried to pull it out from under his head. She didn't mind getting a little hay in her hair, but she wouldn't stand for total wardrobe abuse. It was already a concession that she wasn't wearing heels. But before she could get the coat out from under his head, he wrapped a powerful hand around her waist and tugged her back on top of him.

"You are such a pain," she said lovingly. She stared down into his gorgeous midnight blue eyes and plucked a piece of hay from one of his unruly brown curls. His lips were red and chapped from kissing. So were hers, and it felt glorious. "And no, I'm not in love with scratchy horse blankets."

He placed his hand on her lower back, on top of her strawberry-shaped birthmark. He rested his fingers easily under the waistband of her jeans. "You're like the princess and the pea."

She didn't know about the pea part, but she definitely felt like a princess. The Waverly riding stables could have been a luxury suite at the Ritz-Carlton Atlanta, her governor mother's hotel of choice, for all she cared. The stables were cozy and private—and that was all they needed. Easy had wanted to head up to the bluffs so that they could look out over the Hudson, but they'd abandoned that idea when they spotted the cross-country team running in that direction. Nothing like a team of skinny runner geeks with stopwatches to ruin a romantic, clothing-free afternoon.

"What are you thinking about?" he asked, lifting his head to nibble on her left earlobe. His voice was gentle and sweet. Everything about Easy was familiar. Sometimes he even reminded her of things that had nothing to do with him, like the sweet tea she'd loved as a kid. They didn't have it in the Northeast, and it was one of the only things she missed about the South.

She hadn't been thinking about anything besides him, but now that he'd brought it up, her mind was flooded with the things she probably *should* be thinking about. Like the fact that she'd just bailed on Tinsley and her plan to get Jenny kicked out of Waverly. She'd meant what she'd said on the phone—Tinsley would probably be better off without her. That girl could lie her way through anything, and Callie's nervous fidgeting would only make them seem suspicious.

"I was just thinking . . . about last night." They'd lost their virginity together, and it had been everything she'd ever hoped it would be, with the one person she'd hoped it would be with.

They'd remember it for the rest of their lives. She'd even kept a piece of straw from the barn and put it in her top drawer, so that she'd forever have a memento from their night together. Now that the barn itself was gone, she was glad she'd kept it, and she sort of liked the idea that she had in her possession the only remnant of the place where they'd lost their virginity. She kissed Easy on the cheek and he smiled his half-cocky, half-abashed smile. God, she'd missed that smile. And his smell, like coffee and Marlboro Reds, horses and Ivory soap, and arty paint smells she couldn't really identify. And his knobby knuckles. It was all back now. And all of it was hers.

"Listen." Easy reached up and gently tucked a stray lock of hair behind Callie's ear. He kissed one of the freckles on her neck before leaning back and looking her in the eye. "When I went to the dining hall to get the bagels, I overheard people saying that we might be suspects. Some people think we started the fire." His forehead was creased with worry.

"It's Jenny. She's spreading that rumor everywhere." Callie's face flushed with anger when she thought of the way Jenny had gone off on her last night in their room, accusing her not only of being a horrible friend but of being an irresponsible arsonist. Of course Jenny was just furious about Easy dumping her and was dying for a way to get back at Callie. Not only that, she was just sure Jenny herself had started the fire, out of rage and jealousy. She deserved to get kicked out. And then Callie would have a single. She could rig up a rope ladder and sneak Easy in every night.

"Come on." Easy picked at a brown splotch—paint? something

horsey and disgusting?—on his jeans. "That doesn't really . . . sound like Jenny." His voice was low and soft, as if he were trying to tiptoe around her.

Callie narrowed her hazel eyes, glowering at him. Of course *he* was a Jenny expert. He'd hooked up with her for two fucking weeks and now he knew everything about her? Her back stiffened. She didn't want to have this conversation right now. She didn't want to spend one second thinking about Easy and Jenny. At least Jenny would be out of the picture soon, if Tinsley's meeting with the dean went as planned. If it didn't, there would be plenty of time to remedy the situation, and then she'd never have to think about Jenny again.

"I feel like I owe you a better explanation for what happened with Jenny. Or a better apology. Or something . . ." He trailed off, rubbing his temples with his calloused thumbs. "I mean, there were all these things going on and I just couldn't—"

Callie planted a long, soft kiss on his chapped lips, hoping that would shut him up.

Easy kissed her back, then pulled away slowly. Callie's milky white skin had turned a delicate shade of pink, and he knew that no matter how cool she tried to play it, she was still upset about Jenny. Of course it was a sensitive subject for Callie—it had probably killed her to see him with Jenny, and so it was natural that she'd be angry. But still . . . Jenny didn't deserve to be blamed for the mess he'd made with Callie. "Don't you think we should, uh, talk about it?" He sat up on the blanket and pulled her up with him, pulling her fluffy white coat out from under his head.

"Shhh." Callie put her finger over his lips, then replaced it with her own mouth. The sun had crawled high into the sky, and it cast long shadows all over the stable floor. "We're together now, and that's all that matters."

Easy opened his mouth to speak but she silenced him with a long, slow kiss. Callie was right. They were together again, and this time nothing was going to change the way he felt about her.

5

A WAVERLY OWL DOES NOT TAKE ADVANTAGE

OF PROSPECTIVE OWLS.

Brandon Buchanan lay on his Ralph Lauren bedspread with his squash-calloused hands folded beneath his head. *Mr. Open is closed.* He still couldn't believe that for once in his life, he'd been able to say something that actually sounded like a line from a movie. He was always coming up with good comebacks after the fact, but finally, he'd nailed it. There was something transcendent about the moment. He'd let Elizabeth Jacobs, the hot St. Lucius girl he'd hoped to make his girlfriend, know that if she insisted on keeping her relationships "open"—meaning she still got to flirt and hook up with whoever she wanted, even in front of Brandon—certain Men of Quality wouldn't be available for her anymore. She'd have to settle for a lifetime of guys like Brian Atherton. Atherton. That fucker.

A soft knock interrupted his self-congratulatory meditation.

Maybe it was Elizabeth, there to tell him how sorry she was. That if he wouldn't take her back, she was going to join a convent and forsake all the Athertons of the world and him, forever, or something equally film-like and romantic.

He coughed and attempted a steady, manly voice. "Come in."

But instead of Elizabeth's dirty-blond head, the bearded face of Pierre Hausler, the Canadian dorm supervisor, appeared in the doorway. House, as everyone called him, was one of those Waverly alums who'd arrived as a teenager and then had never left—or, if he had, it had only been long enough to get a college degree. He supervised the dorm, assistant coached the girls' softball team, and taught freshman earth science and recorder. He also said, "Eh?"

"Bad time, eh?" House asked, pausing in the doorway. Despite his nickname, he was a slim guy and looked a bit like Johnny Knoxville with facial hair. He also happened to be pretty cool, never harassing them too much about lights-out. *"Bad time, eh?"* was his signature hello.

"Nah." Brandon sat up, running a hand through his short, wavy dark gold hair. "What's up?"

House pushed the door open farther, revealing a skinny kid Brandon had never seen before. He had spiky light brown hair that looked like it had never seen a comb in its life, and he was holding an army green L.L.Bean sleeping bag with the initials SRT embroidered in orange at the top. He wasn't all that much bigger than Brandon's half brothers, Zach and Luke, who were eleven and still thought Super Soakers were the coolest things in the world. They especially liked to torture

Brandon's Labrador—who, incidentally, was also named Elizabeth. Brandon briefly wondered if, from now on, every time he called his dog, he'd be reminded of his experience with open-minded women.

House stuck a thumb toward the kid. "This is Sam Tri . . . Trigonis." House was notoriously bad with names, which was especially problematic for a dorm adviser—he often referred to his advisees by their room numbers. "He's one of the prospectives visiting this weekend."

Prospectives. With everything that had happened last week—his short, bittersweet fling with Elizabeth, and the insane burning barn last night—Brandon had forgotten there'd be a bunch of little eighth-graders shadowing people around campus for the next few days.

"He was supposed to be staying with Brian Atherton, but there was an, um, incident at the squash courts this morning," House continued. Brandon noticed a dark spot under the kid's eye that stretched to the bridge of his nose. It looked like he'd taken a ball to the face, and hard. House nodded his head of curly dark hair at Brandon. "Sam, this is Brandon Buchanan."

"Nice to meet you." Sam stepped into the room Brandon shared with Heath Ferro, his hand stuck out like a politician's. He wore a black-faded-to-gray Harry Potter T-shirt and khakis with a dorkily neat crease down the front. If he hadn't looked so earnest, it might have been cool. But it wasn't.

"Uh, nice to meet you, too." Brandon swung his Perry Ellis–socked feet to the hardwood floor and leaned forward to shake the kid's hand.

House smiled hopefully at Brandon. "So, you don't mind showing him around a little—maybe taking him somewhere other than the squash courts?" He planted his large hands on Sam's skinny shoulders. "I'll owe you one."

Brandon sighed heavily, and House disappeared back down the hall, leaving the tragically nerdy eighth-grader in the middle of Brandon's room. A pair of brown leather top-siders peeked out from his slightly-too-short khaki pants.

"Nice room," Sam offered shyly. He turned around in a circle, his eyes lighting up when he spotted Heath's PSP on his filthy bed. He looked back at Brandon expectantly, the way Elizabeth (the dog—this could get confusing, he realized) did when she wanted him to throw a stick. Brandon wondered if he could command the eighth-grader with "Sit!" or "Stay!" but only assholes like Ferro treated people like that.

"So, uh, why do you want to go to Waverly?" he asked, smoothing out his navy blue plaid Ralph Lauren bedspread. It seemed like the Waverly handbook thing to say.

"Chicks," Sam answered simply.

Brandon laughed, surprised. "You don't have girls at your school?"

"Teases." Sam set down his sleeping bag on the floor and sat on Heath's unmade bed. He picked up the PSP, flipping it around in his hands and examining it. "All of them." He ran his thumb lovingly over the power button.

"We've got a couple of those at Waverly, too." Brandon nodded sagely. "You can play that, if you want," he added. Sam eagerly flipped it on, and the familiar music of Spider-Man 3 filled the room. "Heath won't mind." Ha. If Heath knew Brandon had let some gawky amateur touch his prized possession, he'd write profanities on Brandon's wall with his favorite Molton Brown pomade. He'd already done it once, freshman year.

"They're *everywhere*," Sam agreed, his thumbs already expertly maneuvering the tiny game console. "But I hear they're hotter here, at least." He tore his eyes away from the screen and turned to Brandon. "Do you have any other games besides Spider-Man 3? I beat this one already."

Brandon ran his hand through his hair, blinking his golden brown eyes. What the hell was he going to do with this nerdy whiz kid all weekend? Cheer him on as he played video games? Compare the merits of high school girls with their eighth-grade equivalents? Just then, the door was kicked open with a bang. Heath stood in the doorway, a giant sweat stain ballooning disgustingly on the front of his gray Ridgefield Prep T-shirt.

"What the—?"

"This is Sam, our prospective student." Brandon wrinkled his nose. Heath smelled like a cross between rotten asparagus and gorgonzola cheese. Didn't he ever wear deodorant? Brandon had once left a brand-new Speed Stick on Heath's bedside table, with a sticky note attached to it that read, "Try this." The next day, the deodorant had disappeared and there was a bottle of Nair sitting on Brandon's bed, with a sticky that read, "Try this—on your privates." Brandon had given up on Heath's hygiene ever since.

"Get off my bed," Heath panted. He peeled off his shirt and tossed it on the floor.

Sam stood up quickly, moving to Brandon's side of the room.

"Would it kill you to take a shower before coming in here?" Brandon grunted as he stood and opened the window. "And do your goddamn laundry—it's growing mold." He wasn't usually this aggressive with Heath, but Sam made for an appreciative audience.

"Maybe you can take it in when you bring your dresses to the cleaners." Heath's green eyes flashed mischievously, and he flexed his biceps in front of his closet mirror, seeming to appreciate what he saw. "Easy on the starch." He finally looked at Sam, who kept touching his swollen nose. "What happened to your grill?"

"I got it caught in a beaver trap," Sam answered defiantly.

Brandon chuckled. This kid had some balls. "Actually, he put his face in front of Atherton's squash racket."

"Too bad then. I like your thinking, though." Heath put his arm around Sam and squeezed him to his bare, sweaty chest. Even though it was mid-October, Heath still had a Caribbean-looking tan. For all his teasing about Brandon's love of products, Brandon had a feeling Heath himself lived by the bottle—of self-tanner. A glow like that took work to maintain. "Waverly chicks love prospectives. I had the *best* experience when I first visited," Heath continued, finally letting go of Sam.

Brandon groaned and threw himself back on his plaid comforter. He carefully pushed his John Varvatos loafers under the bed so Heath or the prospective wouldn't step on them. "Christ, not the Juliet van Pelt story again," he moaned.

"Don't be bitter—it could happen to anyone. Anyone who tries hard enough and really gives it their all." A familiar wistful look had already overtaken Heath as he sat down on his bed, ready to launch into the famed sordid tale.

"It was one of the hottest falls on record here in Rhinecliff," he began, lying back and putting his hands behind his head. He sniffed his armpit, as if to remind himself of his manliness, and continued. "I was young, not much older than you are. I was still paying college kids in 7-Eleven parking lots to buy me *Penthouse* and *Playboy*."

Brandon rolled his eyes, but Heath didn't notice. He gazed wistfully up at the crown molding where the white ceiling met the off-white wall.

"She was the first girl I laid eyes on. And after that, I couldn't look anywhere else. She was playing Frisbee with her friends in this tiny yellow bikini, leaping in the air like a sexy gazelle with the nicest tits I've ever seen. She was like the girls in my magazine dreams, but real. *Juliet van Pelt*." Heath shook his head of dirty-blond hair, as if the sound of her name alone was descriptive of the experience.

Sam took a seat on the bare floor, leaning back against Brandon's bed and watching Heath in awe. Brandon got up and went to the closet to grab his Dunlop squash racket. He might need to smack Heath with it if things got really out of hand.

"I knew exactly what I had to do. Time stopped as the Frisbee flew in the air. I intercepted it and walked straight up to her. I showed no fear. I told her that if she wanted her Frisbee back, she'd need to give me something in return." Heath sat up on his bed, his face gravely serious. He locked eyes with Sam. "And she did. She made a man out of me that night. I'll never forget her."

"Are you for real?" Sam's nerdy face lit up with admiration. He looked like an orphan who'd discovered he had a father after all.

"Yes." Heath rubbed his stubbly chin and nodded wisely, as if he were a Buddhist monk and Sam had trekked halfway across the world to consult him. "You're going to get some this weekend. It'll change your life." His eyes took on that faraway look again. "I'm the man I am today because of that one wonderful night."

It was almost like a bad teen movie. If only it were true. Brandon didn't believe for half a second that thirteen-year-old Heath had somehow managed to walk straight up to a hot senior and convince her to sleep with him within moments of arriving at Waverly.

"You down?" Heath asked, kicking off one of his muddy Adidas sneakers so that it landed right in Sam's lap. He didn't seem to mind.

"I'm down," Sam answered so excitedly it looked like he might wet himself.

Girlish giggling erupted on the sidewalk below, and Heath jumped up and stuck his head out the window. "Love for sale!" he sang at the top of his lungs. "Dirty, nasty love for sale!" The freshmen shrieked in delight and scurried away. Brandon leaned back against his Tempur-Pedic pillow and tried to ignore the disaster-waiting-to-happen playing out before his very eyes. Heath? Coaching a prospective student? In *anything*?

Heath pulled Sam to his feet and over to the window. "Whatever you do, don't settle on a freshman. They don't know anything," he counseled his protégé. "*That's* more like it." He pointed at someone else down below, but Brandon couldn't see. "Hey, ladies," Heath called out.

"They're giving you the bird," Sam whispered, nudging Heath's bare ribs with his elbow.

"It's all part of the elaborate mating ritual," Heath whispered back. "It's not about me, ladies," he yelled down to the poor girls. "Sam here is looking for love and he's come to the *master*."

"You mean mastur*bator*," a feminine voice called up, loud enough for everyone to hear. Brandon couldn't help cracking up. He laid his squash racket over his face, chuckling.

"Hey, that's *sex* with someone I love," Sam shouted back. He turned to Heath. "That's from *Annie Hall*. It's my dad's favorite movie. I've seen it like nine times."

"No, no, no, no." Heath grabbed Sam by his Harry Potter shirt and pulled him away from the window. "You can't do *movie* lines with girls," Heath warned. "They never catch them, so it's just a waste of time." He strode over to his closet and glanced back over his shoulder at Sam, who looked like he wished he had a notebook in which to write it all down. "You've got lots to learn, and we haven't much time."

He grabbed a fresh shirt and led Sam down the hall, launching into a lecture about how it was important to be funny and articulate, but not too articulate, hence the genius of one-liners.

Brandon lay back down on the bed with a sigh, glad to have

the room all to himself again. He was tired of smelly, loud Heath Ferro, his far-out stories of sexual conquests, and his romantic tutelage. But then again, he wasn't having much success on his own. Maybe he could use some lessons, from a girl who knew a little more about the birds and the bees than he did. The campus was full of them. He just had to find the right one.

OwlNet

AlisonQuentin: It's eleven o'clock on Saturday night—do you know where your children are?

AlanStGirard: Things are creepy-quiet on campus, huh?

AlisonQuentin: Guess everyone's laying low b/c of last night?

AlanStGirard: I wouldn't mind laying low on your pillow. . . .

AlisonQuentin: Ur bad.

AlanStGirard: Is that a yes?

AlisonQuentin: Obviously.

A WAVERLY OWL KNOWS FRIENDSHIP MEANS
OCCASIONALLY HAVING TO SAY YOU'RE SORRY.

Sunday afternoon, Callie strode briskly across the freshly
mowed quad, wishing she could outwalk the pesky prospective student who had been attached to her hip since
brunch. Her black Lanvin pumps were sinking into the grass,
but taking the gravel path would only prolong the walk to
Dumbarton, and she wanted to get rid of Chloe as soon as possible. She spotted another young-looking girl reading a book
under a tree and thought about shoving Chloe in that direction
and telling her to go make a friend.

"So," Chloe panted, clearly struggling to keep up with
Callie's long strides. The ivy-covered campus was in full autumn
bloom, the normally green vines climbing the distinguished
brick buildings now tinged with red. The girls' legs kicked
up fallen leaves as they walked. "What's going to happen to
whoever they catch?"

Callie pulled a tissue from her dove gray Helmut Lang jacket and pretended to blow her nose. *Alison* was the one who had volunteered to show this kid around Waverly, but she had abruptly stood up in the middle of brunch, told everyone she was off to "study" with Alan, and shoved her prospective on Benny and Sage. When they'd announced they were going to do shots in their room, Chloe had asked timidly where she should go. In a moment of weakness, Callie had offered to take her around for a little while.

That didn't mean she had to keep her forever, though, did it?

"I don't know." Callie stuffed the tissue back into her pocket. Her white Elie Tahari miniskirt was creeping up a little on her thighs as she walked, and she wanted to change, but she didn't want to take Chloe back to her room unless it was absolutely necessary. She wasn't exactly dressed appropriately for mid-October weather, but it was her first appearance in the dining hall since the fire—and her and Easy's half-naked emergence from the barn—and she'd wanted to look her clothed best. "They'll probably get expelled, or arrested . . . or both."

Callie was feeling tired today. She and Easy had spent all day and into the night yesterday in various Waverly hookup spots. To avoid talking about Jenny or the fire, Callie had adopted an all-sex, no-talk policy with Easy, at least for the time being. Not that it was too much of a hardship. But the fact that they couldn't just hang out in their dorm rooms made it a bit exhausting. She'd signed up for a boyfriend, not Outward Bound.

"Would they go to prison?" Chloe asked, almost jogging to keep up as Callie strode in between two sophomore guys playing catch. She wore a hunter green turtleneck sweater, and Callie had to fight the urge to take the extra fabric at the neck and pull it over the prospective's head so she'd shut up already.

"I don't know." She flashed a smile at the cuter of the two boys as they obediently held their Nerf football until she and Chloe had passed, and she felt their eyes watch her walk away. Nothing like a gorgeous boyfriend to do wonders for a girl's confidence.

"Or maybe just do community service?"

Did this girl ever shut up? "I don't know." Not that it would be the worst thing in the world to have Jenny locked away in prison in one of those bright orange jumpsuits that would look terrible with her complexion. Tinsley had reported back to Callie that her meeting with the dean had been a failure, but that hadn't seemed to deter her. In the meantime, they were both supposed to be coming up with a plan B. Distracted by Easy, Callie hadn't exactly been focusing on their mission. She knew Tinsley would be disappointed in her total lack of guile.

"Yo, C.V.!" Callie turned to see Tinsley standing behind her. Speak of the devil. She looked perky in a short Nike tennis dress, the body-hugging fabric startlingly white against her perfect tan. Her black, Pantene Pro-V commercial-shiny hair was pulled into a tight ponytail at the crown of her head. "Who's this?" Tinsley pointed her Wilson tennis racket accusingly at Chloe, who shrank into herself as if she were at knifepoint. But Callie couldn't help but notice that Chloe was gazing admiringly at Tinsley. Callie rolled her eyes. Was there anyone, guy or girl, who didn't worship Tinsley—even as they stood in fear of her?

"Prospective," Callie replied evenly. "Chloe, meet Tinsley."

Tinsley squinted her violet eyes, sizing up the girl. "You look really familiar," she said. "Have you visited Waverly before?"

Chloe shook her pale blond head quietly, seemingly shell-shocked that the great Tinsley Carmichael was actually talking to her. Whatever.

"Tins, I'll see you later," Callie said, eager to get to Dumbarton and foist Chloe on the first person she saw.

"Later." Tinsley saluted the girls with her tennis racket and headed in the direction of the courts. Callie pounded up the front steps to Dumbarton and threw open the door, looking around for her unlucky victim.

Except . . . the lobby was mysteriously empty, even for a Sunday. With its buttery leather couches and ground-floor windows, the common room was usually filled with girls eating burned popcorn and watching movies, or pretending to hold study groups as they gossiped over their open textbooks. It was never this quiet. It was like those eerie scenes in horror movies where everyone else is already dead and the killer is just waiting for the right time to launch his final attack.

But then Callie spotted a pair of pink ladybug-covered socks hanging off the side of the plush leather couch. Brett was listening to her iPod, her pointy nose wedged in her tattered paperback copy of *The Catcher in the Rye*. Brett sometimes picked up the book and started reading it in the middle, or at the end.

Brett called Callie "Stradlater," Holden Caulfield's pain-in-the-ass roommate. Or she used to anyway. These days they hardly talked.

Callie was about to tug on Brett's socked foot, but the memory of drunkenly spilling the beans about Brett and Kara to the entire Waverly campus flooded her brain. Looking at Brett in her silly socks, reading her favorite book, she felt awful. Did Brett know it was Callie's fault?

Brett turned the page and jumped at the sight of Callie. She pulled out an earbud, and Callie could hear Nine Inch Nails spilling out.

"Hey," Brett said coolly, her green eyes flashing. She crossed her arms over her chest. "Come to tell more of my deepest, darkest secrets to the whole school?"

Well, that answered that. "Hey." Callie didn't know what else to say.

Brett's lips were a glossy red, making her alabaster skin look even paler. She was really getting shit on this year, Callie thought, between the Mr. Dalton disaster, Jeremiah sleeping with someone else, and then the whole everyone-talking-about-her-being-a-lesbian thing.

Callie tried to apologize with her eyes. "I . . . was . . . wondering if you'd mind taking Chloe." Callie hoped it came out like a request and not a demand.

"Who's Chloe?" Brett asked, confused. She sat up on the couch, tugging at the bottom of her frayed white C&C V-neck.

Callie spun around. Chloe was gone. "She was just here. . . ."

"New roommate?" Brett arched her eyebrows.

Callie laughed. After the Jenny disaster, they didn't need any new roommates. "No, she's a prospective. I got her from Sage and Benny. Maybe she went to the bathroom," she added with a shrug. Brett fidgeted with her iPod while Callie loomed over the couch. Finally, she plopped down on the overstuffed easy chair across from Brett. She played with the zipper of her jacket, tugging it up and down, and took a deep breath. "Look, I wanted to apologize about Friday night. I was drunk, which I know is no excuse, but you know I would normally never, like, tell a secret like that."

Brett was stone-faced, and Callie prepared herself for an angry tirade.

"I guess I just, well, I don't know," she continued in a rush. She put her hands in her pockets and instantly took them out, remembering the dirty tissue. "I know I shouldn't have said anything. It was an awful thing to do and I'm really sorry. If I could take it back, I would." It wasn't the most eloquent statement in the world, but as soon as she'd said it, Callie felt a weight lift. She knew she could never say anything that would undo the damage done by leaking Brett's secret, but there was some small salvation in saying she was sorry. And meaning it. She was terrible at apologizing—but right now, all she really wanted was to make things better with Brett.

"It's okay." Brett shrugged, toying with a piece of Crayola-red hair. "I'm actually sort of over caring what people think, anyway." She sized up Callie, as if determining Callie's level of sincerity. "Anyway, I forgive you."

Callie felt tears well up in her eyes, and she wanted to leap up and hug Brett, but then she heard Chloe's New Balance sneakers padding across the hardwood floors.

Callie jerked her head toward the approaching pre-frosh. "This is Chloe." She met Brett's sharp, cat-like green eyes and gave her a "so sorry" look.

Brett set the small white book down on her lap and waved her sparkly gold nails at Chloe.

"I love that book." Chloe stared at her sneakered feet shyly as she spoke.

"Me, too," Brett agreed, smiling.

Excellent. They already had something in common. Callie stood up to go, pulling her miniskirt down and hoping she hadn't flashed the prospective, Britney Spears–style. "Do you mind?"

Brett rolled her eyes at Callie, but she could tell she didn't really mind. "It's fine. She can stay with me."

"Thanks." Callie turned and whisked down the hall, her heels clicking as she walked, propelled by Brett's forgiveness.

She was back with Easy, and she and Brett were friends again. Things were almost back to normal. Almost. Now, if she and Tinsley could just make Jenny Humphrey disappear, all would be right with the world again.

A WAVERLY OWL TAKES IT UPON HERSELF TO
ENTERTAIN AND EDUCATE PROSPECTIVE OWLS.

Brett walked, sock-footed, down the polished hardwood halls of Dumbarton, with Chloe trailing behind her. The prospective was talking nonstop about Holden lying to his parents and running around New York City after he'd been kicked out of boarding school. "Has anyone at Waverly ever done anything like that?" she asked.

"Uh, I don't think so." Brett glanced over her shoulder at the petite pre-frosh, who reminded her a little bit of Reese Witherspoon in *Election,* one of her favorite movies. Reese played an ambitious, seemingly straight-edge girl who ran for class president and wound up playing dirty to get what she wanted. But Chloe seemed way too sweet and innocent to do anything like that, especially given the incredulous look in her wide blue eyes at even the talk of running around New York unchaperoned.

It was something Brett had kind of fantasized about—getting kicked out of Waverly, and instead of heading home to her parents' gargantuan house on the Jersey shore, living on the lam in Manhattan, staying in hotels by herself and getting drunk in dirty bars with bohemian writers and artists. There was something totally glamorous about it.

Except not really. Her parents would probably track her down, kill her, and dress her in zebra print for her own funeral. No, thank you.

As they rounded a corner, Brett noticed that Kara's door was open a crack, just enough to allow the scent of a strawberry candle and the fading chords of a Shins song to leak out into the hall. Brett smiled. She and Kara had spent all day yesterday lazing around in Kara's room, reading comic books and watching DVDs on her laptop, occasionally pausing to kiss. After twenty-four hours of lying low, away from all her whispering classmates, she was feeling much better about everything. With Chloe on her heels, they wouldn't exactly have alone time, but being with Kara was better than dealing with the girl on her own.

Brett didn't pause to knock, and strode through the doorway. The room was characteristically neat and slightly barren. She had no idea how Kara kept her desk so clean—all it had on it was a closed laptop and a cup of pens. Kara was curled on her side on her Batgirl comforter, her head resting on her bare arm, the brightly colored pages of a comic book open in front of her. The Shins song had finished, and a Decembrists song Brett could never remember the name of was now filtering through the speakers of Kara's iPod docking station.

"Hey." Kara smiled as she took in Brett, raising her head slowly. She sat up and tugged down her charcoal gray T-shirt. The word BROOKLYN was screen-printed across it in uneven cursive, and Brett remembered how Kara had promised to take her down to Dumbo to visit her up-and-coming fashion designer mom's loft studio. She wondered briefly how Kara would introduce her if they ever went. *Hey Mom, meet my new girlfriend?*

"Smelled the candle a mile away—you know Pardee would love to bust you for that." Brett gestured toward the candle on the nightstand. Candles were banned in dorm rooms, and Angelica Pardee, Dumbarton's live-in dorm adviser, was notorious for unexpectedly appearing at girls' doors and slapping violation notices into their hands. Brett suspected she had an entire cabinet full of half-burned candles that she gleefully lighted herself while taking bubble baths and drinking cheap merlot.

"The candle was more powerful than advertised," Kara explained, throwing her legs off her bed and leaning over the nightstand. She cupped one hand behind the flame and blew it out, tiny smoke vapors rising up to the ceiling. "It was supposed to be 'lightly scented.'"

"It smells like Pop-Tarts," Chloe piped up, stepping onto the off-white woven rug in the center of the room.

Kara leaned back on her elbows and cracked the half smile that Brett loved. It made her look like she knew something you didn't. She stuck her hands in the pockets of her faded black Diesel jeans. "Who's this?"

"This is Chloe, one of the prospectives."

"Nice to meet you, Chloe." Kara folded her legs up beneath her and gestured toward the bed. Chloe didn't need to be asked twice and immediately sat down on the mattress, her feet dangling off the edge. Brett dropped into the beanbag chair in the corner.

"So how do you like Waverly?" Kara took a yellow plastic barrette from the drawer in her nightstand and secured a stray piece of her light brown hair, pulling it away from her face. Brett always thought it was impressive when girls could do their hair without looking in a mirror.

"It's pretty cool." Chloe picked up the *X-Men* comic and leafed through it. Yesterday, Kara had insisted that Magneto was cuter than Wolverine. Brett smiled, remembering how adamant Kara had been. "Everyone here seems really . . . cool."

"You clearly haven't met everyone then," Kara answered wryly, and Brett laughed.

"It sure feels like I have," Chloe said, a little sadly. She put down the comic book and pushed her rectangular-framed glasses up on her nose.

"What do you mean?" Brett asked. She stared at a framed black-and-white photo of a young, bushy-haired Bob Dylan holding a sign that said LOOK OUT.

"I mean, I've been walking around campus, being passed from one person to another. . . ." Chloe crossed her arms. "No one wants me around."

"That's harsh," Kara said, shuffling past an Iron & Wine song on the iPod that made Brett think of Jeremiah and the night they'd almost slept together. Was her whole life going to be like this now, avoiding certain songs or music that reminded her of her mistakes? Billie Holiday made her think of Eric Dalton; Iron & Wine was Jeremiah; and if things didn't work out with Kara, she'd never be able to listen to Bob Dylan again. By the time she reached her twenties, she'd be a huge, lumbering mass of musical baggage.

"I guess I missed a great party on Friday night, huh?" Chloe blurted. "Were you guys there when the barn caught fire?"

"We were all there." Kara grabbed the comic book and flipped through the pages nonchalantly, as if fires happened at Waverly all the time.

"Were you inside? Did you have to run for your lives?" Chloe's eyes widened excitedly, and she bounced a little on the bed.

Brett laughed and leaned back in the beanbag. She was feeling more relaxed by the minute. She had overreacted on Saturday and was glad she hadn't voiced her worries to Kara. With everyone obsessing over the fire, who even cared about a little thing like two girls kissing? "If we'd been in it, we'd be dead."

"I heard some people were in it," Chloe said matter-of-factly, leaning her back against the wall behind Kara's bed.

"Like who?" Brett shifted again in the beanbag. She'd never noticed how uncomfortable it was. It was like sitting on a bag of frozen peas.

The prospective gave a winsome Mona Lisa smile. "You know. A bunch of people: Easy and Callie and Jenny and this guy Heath, and also some guy named Julie or something like that."

Kara laughed and threw her head back on her pillow.

"What?" Chloe looked hurt.

"Julian," Kara corrected her. "His name is Julian."

Chloe's face reddened. "Well, that's what I heard anyway. I guess I didn't hear it right."

"I doubt *all* those people were *in* the barn," Brett noted casually. Jenny? She hadn't really seen Jenny around this weekend, although Brett had been kind of keeping to herself. Or rather, spending time alone with Kara. "We were having a movie party on the lawn around the barn. The fire was just an accident."

"They found a lighter that belongs to one of the students." Chloe shook her head vigorously, her feathery blond hair fluttering around her shoulders. "Arson," she added in a whisper.

Brett looked at Kara, who mouthed the word *wow*. Clearly, Chloe *had* met nearly everyone on campus, and she had overheard quite a bit.

"There might've been some people in the barn," Kara said, tapping her fingernails against the wooden headboard. "There were probably people in and out of it all night. You know, hooking up and stuff." She raised her eyebrows suggestively at Brett, and Brett blushed.

Luckily, Chloe didn't seem to notice. She hopped up and started looking through Kara's white Ikea bookshelf. All the dorm rooms had been fitted with standard furnishings: a bed, a dresser, a desk, a bookshelf, and a wooden chair with the

Waverly crest on it—but Kara somehow seemed to have her own furniture. "You've got a lot of books." Chloe traced her hand across the long line of alphabetized titles. "What's this about?" she asked, pulling out a copy of Virginia Woolf's *Mrs. Dalloway*.

Kara smiled wickedly and glanced at Brett. "Well, it's about two women who love each other but can't be together because of the society they live in." Kara reached for the ChapStick she always kept in the top drawer of her nightstand and put some on her pink lips. They looked totally kissable. "They're forced into loveless marriages instead."

"Oh," Chloe said, looking a little startled. She held the book at a distance from her body, like it might burn her.

"You can borrow it if you want," Kara offered, a glint in her green-brown eyes. Brett had to stifle a giggle. Chloe was sweet and all, but Kara had the right idea—if they made her uncomfortable enough, maybe she'd leave and they could be alone together.

Chloe blushed and put the book back on the shelf. "That's okay."

"Maybe it's time to go find Alison," Brett said pointedly, looking at Chloe.

"Where'd she go?" Kara asked. Brett mouthed Alan's name. "Oh, right." Kara nodded. "She did have to *study*."

Chloe seemed a bit crestfallen. "Okay, yeah," she agreed, stepping away from the bookshelf. She looked like a puppy that was being ushered inside while its siblings played in the yard.

Brett followed Chloe to the door, practically pushing her out through it. "You can find your way to Alison's room, right?" She didn't wait for the girl's answer and pulled the door shut, turning to grin at Kara. She was glad they didn't live in Virginia Woolf's time.

A WAVERLY OWL KNOWS PROSPECTIVES HAVE THEIR USES.

Brandon threw off his sweaty Nike squash shirt and tossed it into his white Pottery Barn hamper. His laundry pile was mounting by the day. He normally used Waverly's Fluff n' Fold service, but in all the recent insanity he hadn't managed to drop a load off for a while. At least the room was quiet now that Heath was squiring Sam all over the campus, making him over in his image. As if one Heath Ferro wasn't enough. Soon there would be two. Brandon had an image of feeding them after midnight and watching a thousand sleazy Ferros spread over the school, like Gremlins.

He reached for his Acqua di Gio deodorant and swiped some under each armpit. He hadn't been able to stop obsessing over Elizabeth since yesterday—he'd begun to doubt that he'd made the right decision in telling her off—and had gone to the squash courts this afternoon to try to burn off some of his nervous energy. He knew that as soon as he met someone new, Elizabeth would be a thing of the past. But given the drought of decent girls at Waverly, he might be subjected to a fate of over-thinking and furious squash playing, at least for the foreseeable future.

There was a timid knock on the door, and Brandon walked over to the wooden dresser. He hoped he could get a fresh shirt on before Sam burst in and started teasing him, Ferro style, about shaving his chest. "Come in," he said, and before he could even choose a shirt from the drawer, the door opened.

"Are you Alan's roommate?" A smallish blond girl with wide-set blue eyes stood in Brandon's doorway, looking around. When her eyes caught Brandon's bare, sweaty chest, they widened slightly.

Brandon automatically held the T-shirt in front of his body. He wasn't exactly modest—he'd started lifting regularly, in an attempt to outmuscle Julian McCafferty, the squash team's newest member and the first threat to Brandon's reign in three years. He was looking pretty muscled of late, if he said so himself, and even Elizabeth had noticed. But this girl couldn't have been more than thirteen, and it seemed sort of wrong to be half naked in front of her.

"You mean Alan St. Girard? He lives with Easy Walsh, down the hall. Why are you—" But before Brandon could finish his sentence, a loud whooping noise interrupted from behind the girl.

"Brandon, my man, getting on that fresh meat!" Heath stormed into the room with Sam on his heels and put a hand up in the air for Brandon to slap. Brandon kept his hands on the clean T-shirt, and Heath slapped hands with Sam instead.

"She's looking for Alan," Brandon grumbled. "Christ, she's probably not even thirteen yet," he added under his breath. "Why are you looking for Alan, anyway?" He turned to the girl, who was fidgeting with the hem of her dark green turtleneck sweater and seemed to have fixed her gaze on Sam. Not that Sam noticed. The prospective had plopped down on Heath's messy bed and was already tuned into the PSP.

"I'm staying with Alison Quentin, but I went to her room and she wasn't there, so her roommate told me to try the boys' dorm. She's studying with Alan."

"Studying, huh?" Heath cackled, popping up the collar of his red Polo shirt in amusement. Sam was wearing an identical one, though it looked about three sizes too big. "I've done a lot of *studying* in my day." He reached out to slap another high five with Sam, but the boy was too engrossed in his game to notice.

"I'm Chloe, by the way," the girl piped up, taking a step farther into the room. She stole a glance at Sam again, but he still hadn't seemed to notice her. Probably because of Heath's programming, Brandon thought—he'd told the kid not to waste time with freshman girls, and no doubt he'd ruled out prospectives unilaterally.

"Listen, Chloe." Brandon felt a bit bad for the girl. She was probably totally lost on campus and didn't need Ferro teasing her. He'd be amazed if any of the prospectives decided to come to Waverly after meeting his abrasive roommate. "Maybe it would be best if you—"

"If you took your shirt off!" Heath cried. "Has Brandon told you about the naked rule? Or is he just trying to teach by example?" Heath quickly ripped his polo off over the top of his head, exposing his muscled, fake 'n' bake chest.

Brandon was sure Chloe was going to gasp and then make a break for it, but she held her ground in the doorway, seemingly unfazed by Heath's sudden half-naked state.

"You see, my dear," Heath continued, grabbing at Sam's shirt and trying to pull it off, "We have a no-shirts policy in this room, and if you don't comply with it, we're going to have to ask you to leave." His eyes gleamed devilishly, and he continued to yank at Sam's shirt while Sam mumbled, "Quit it," and stared down at the game.

Chloe narrowed her eyes at Heath. "I don't think that's in the Waverly handbook," she said challengingly. She put her hands on her hips, and Brandon was momentarily reminded of Callie when she was annoyed and didn't want to take any bullshit. Who would have guessed this girl had that kind of spunk?

"It's not." Heath shrugged in a you-can't-fight-city-hall kind of way. "But Brandon here feels *very* strongly about it. Don't you, Brandon?" With sudden inspiration, Heath stuck his head out the open window and cried, "Naked party in Heath and Brandon's room!" at the top of his lungs.

Chloe just shook her head. "You guys are so immature. I can't believe such pretty girls have crushes on you."

Heath turned, taking a sudden interest in Chloe. "What girls? What girls, what girls, *what girls?*" He leaped across the room and lay prostrate at Chloe's feet, tugging at the hem of her sweater. "You have to tell me!"

The prospective just rolled her eyes and batted Heath's hands off of her. "Well, I overheard Sage Francis saying she thought Brandon was cute," she said, looking at Brandon disapprovingly. "But God, I'm going to tell her not to bother!" And with that, she turned on her heel and stormed out. As she clomped off down the hall, Brandon thought he heard her mutter, "And I thought eighth-grade boys were bad!" Poor girl. She still didn't know what room Alan lived in, and who knew what awaited her behind any of the doors in a dorm full of teenage boys.

Brandon pulled his clean shirt on over his head thoughtfully. Sage Francis? She was pretty cute, although he'd never really thought of her that way before.

Heath was rolling on the floor like a dog, laughing, and Sam, now shirtless, was still engrossed in his game of Spider-Man. Maybe he should try talking to Sage Francis, Brandon thought. It had to be better than hanging out here.

From: DeanMarymount@waverly.edu
To: BrandonBuchanan@waverly.edu
              TinsleyCarmichael@waverly.edu
              BennyCunningham@waverly.edu
              SageFrancis@waverly.edu
              JennyHumphrey@waverly.edu
              JulianMcCafferty@waverly.edu
              BrettMesserschmidt@waverly.edu
              AlisonQuentin@waverly.edu
              CallieVernon@waverly.edu
              EasyWalsh@waverly.edu
              KaraWhalen@waverly.edu
Date: Monday, October 14, 8:46 A.M.
Subject: Disciplinary Meeting

Dear Students,

If you are receiving this e-mail, that means you have been placed
on a short list of suspects responsible for Friday night's reckless and
dangerous barn fire. Your attendance is required at a mandatory
meeting in my office in Stansfield Hall on Wednesday at 8 A.M.

No exceptions.

Dean Marymount

SageFrancis: Shit has hit the fan!

BennyCunningham: Since when are we as suspicious as Easy and Callie? Or Tinsley? And Julian? Hello, lighter?

SageFrancis: Whatevah. Looking forward to being locked in the DC room with Brandon . . .

BennyCunningham: Uh, yeah. And the 11 other suspects. Très romantic.

SageFrancis: If we go to prison, there are always conjugal visits!

OwlNet

KaraWhalen: Ohmigod, how did we end up on the list?

BrettMesserschmidt: No clue. Guilty by association??

KaraWhalen: Since when did Waverly become a totalitarian regime? And can our junior prefect really be a suspect?

BrettMesserschmidt: Dunno, but I'm about to find out.

A WAVERLY OWL SHOWS GRACE UNDER FIRE.

Jenny made her way through the coffee bar inside Maxwell Hall on Monday morning, her attention locked on the close-to-spilling mocha cappuccino in her hands. She turned away from the counter and scanned the crowded café area for an empty table. The main entryway of Maxwell was like that of a castle, with Romanesque arches cut out of its tall stone walls. Jenny loved to sit in the dark alcoves on the upper tier, where you could quietly read a book or watch everyone who came in and out of the café area. But as she scanned around for a seat, she had the distinct impression that everyone was staring at her. She blinked hard, wondering if she was being paranoid. Her thick gray cable-knit J.Crew stockings and brown cord skirt were totally Monday A.M. appropriate. And she'd just woken up, so there was nothing in her teeth. She sighed. In her month at Waverly, people had found some new reason to stare at her almost every day. For being new and clueless, for being big-chested, for stupidly making out with Heath Ferro, for getting caught with Easy in her bed (innocently), for hooking up with Easy (less innocently), for getting dumped by Easy (totally innocently), and now . . . for *what*?

She spotted Sage and Benny at a round wooden table against the wall, near one of the large fireplaces. Jenny moved toward them, but they were so engrossed in conversation they didn't seem to notice her.

"No matter what?" Sage asked, her hand clutching at the sleeve of Benny's navy-striped Le Tigre hoodie.

"No matter what." Benny flicked at Sage's wrist. "Don't get all clutchy on me."

"No matter what, what?" Jenny asked as she pulled out a cushy armchair at their table, careful not to spill her coffee.

Sage and Benny froze.

"What's going on?" Jenny set her giant mug down on the table, which was littered with napkins and a field of pale blue Equal packets.

"The e-mail," Sage whispered dramatically. Wearing a black Ella Moss wrap dress, with gigantic Bottega Veneta sunglasses perched on her head, she looked like a starlet hiding out from the paparazzi. She glanced over her shoulder, but life seemed to be going on as usual in the coffee bar.

"What e-mail?" Jenny took a small sip of her mocha, confused. Had she missed another mildly pornographic e-mail from Heath? Her heart sank a little. Not that she wanted any pornographic e-mail from Heath, but she didn't want to be the only one not included.

"Your name was on it." Benny's aubergine-lined eyes narrowed at Jenny, as if she were trying to catch her in a lie.

"I didn't check my e-mail this morning." Jenny shrugged her small shoulders, glancing at the red plastic wristwatch she'd bought in Chinatown. The numbers were in Chinese. What was with everyone this morning? "What was it, some kind of joke?"

"It's not a joke," Sage answered, pulling a lock of her pale blond hair up to her mouth and looking like she wanted to chew on it. "Someone is going to get kicked out. It could be any of us."

"*Wait.*" Jenny focused on what Sage and Benny were trying to tell her. "Start from the beginning." Benny laid out the gist of Marymount's e-mail, sounding like she knew it by heart, while Sage ticked off the list of Marymount's suspects. Jenny held her stomach when Sage pointed at her and said, "And you, too."

"Probably because they found Julian's lighter," Benny pointed out, stuffing a burgundy Moleskine-bound notebook back into her Fendi tote bag. "And everyone knows about you and Julian."

Jenny put her mug down on the table. They *did*? That was news to Jenny, though she didn't know why she should be surprised, even if there was barely anything to know. Yet.

Benny continued, tapping her chewed-off nails against the oak tabletop. "Which means Marymount probably knows, too. So that's probably why you're on it."

Jenny nodded, staring out the enormous glass windows at the brightly colored treetops, wondering if all other boarding schools had this much drama, or if she was just lucky. Or rather, unlucky.

"Marymount has it in for us because of the candles," Sage explained, flicking invisible dots of Equal off the bell sleeve of her dress.

Benny nodded. "We have a stack of violations. What's the big deal? I smelled someone burning a strawberry candle yesterday. It stank up the entire dorm. These days, everyone has candles but us." She leaned back in the giant armchair and shook her head at the injustice.

Jenny sipped her mochaccino, hoping Benny and Sage's blasé attitude would rub off on her. She wasn't sure this had anything to do with Julian. On Friday night, when she'd confronted Callie about sneaking around with Easy, Callie had snapped back that Jenny had probably started the fire herself. After all, Jenny had more motive than anyone, at least according to Callie's twisted logic. But even if Callie were to go to the dean with that theory, he'd never believe her. Right?

She suddenly remembered how Miss Rosovsky, her American history teacher at Constance Billard, had shown them the historical inaccuracies in the movie *JFK*, but pointed out that most people chose to believe the conspiracy theories anyway. People preferred the more intricate, juicier explanation to the simpler, more logical one. Jenny had a feeling Dean Marymount was one of those people who believed the conspiracies. He didn't want the truth—that the fire was probably an accident. He wanted someone with a motive. He'd prefer to believe that innocent, boarding-school-loving Jenny Humphrey had started it because she was a woman scorned.

"Where are you going?" Benny called out, but Jenny was already exiting the coffee bar door, her kids' size destroyed red Vans heavy and solid against the marble floor of Maxwell Hall.

JennyHumphrey: Hey there . . . just got Dean M's e-mail. Isn't it crazy?

JulianMcCafferty: Totally. You're too beautiful to be a suspect.

JennyHumphrey: I'm blushing. At least we're in it together.

JulianMcCafferty: That's the spirit.

JennyHumphrey: So what are you up to?

JulianMcCafferty: Actually, I was just thinking about you. . . .

JennyHumphrey: Good things, I hope.

JulianMcCafferty: Nope. Bad . . . very bad things.

JennyHumphrey: No wonder we're in trouble. =)

From: HeathFerro@waverly.edu
To: Heath's list of cool people
Date: Monday, October 14, 2:32 P.M.
Subject: Last Chance for US

Goodbye, Brandon, Tinsley, Benny, Sage, Jenny, Julian, Brett, Alison, Callie, Easy, Kara—we'll miss you! (Hell, we'll miss me, too.)

Just in case one of us/some of us/all of us US's (i.e., Usual Suspects) gets handed a one-way ticket away from Waverly on Wednesday morning, I thought we should have a fittingly appropriate going-away party on Tuesday night at the crater. Who knows, it may be our last chance to misbehave here at good ol' Waverly!

Those on Dean M's favorite list—be sure to pick up your hot-off-the-presses US T-shirts at the entry to the party.

Btw, plebes—you're all welcome to the party, to help give US a fond farewell, but whenever you come across one of US, you have to do *exactly* what that person says, as it could be his or her last night of freedom.

Don't mess with US!!

Peace out,

Heath

HeathFerro:	You in for the US party?
TinsleyCarmichael:	I'm there. But I promise you, I won't be leaving the next day.
HeathFerro:	That's the fighting spirit.
TinsleyCarmichael:	Um, you texted me—why?
HeathFerro:	I know you like your guys young . . . but how young?
TinsleyCarmichael:	Listen, Heath. These annoying IMs? I'm starting to hope YOU don't return.
HeathFerro:	Ouch!

A WAVERLY OWL DOES NOT CONSPIRE AGAINST
FELLOW OWLS.

Callie hunched over her chipped yellow cappuccino mug, her bare elbows sticking to the corner booth table at the Waverly Inn in downtown Rhinecliff. It seemed like a million years ago since she and Tinsley and Brett had congregated at this very table over amaretto sours and champagne, in an effort to help her drown out any memory of Easy. The Waverly Inn had seemed like the perfect set for a movie, with its dark wood bar, crusty bartender, and ancient, absurdly proper New England-y style. Today, in the late-morning light, the hotel bar looked more like a cafeteria in an old folks' home. The only patrons were senior citizens, all of whom looked like they'd seen better days. The table was sticky and looked like it needed a good scrub-down, and the chips in the coffee mugs were clear in the light of day.

Class that morning had been out of the question. On Friday,

Mr. Gaston had promised them a "surprise" for Monday, which Callie was pretty sure meant a quiz and not a five-hundred-dollar gift certificate to Barneys. No way could she be expected to identify Latin vocab after Dean Marymount's e-mail. When she first saw the message in her inbox, so quickly after his last one, she'd hoped that the dean had ferreted out the guilty party—i.e., Jenny Humphrey—kicked her out, and closed the case. She'd already mentally planned taking over Jenny's side of the room. But when she found out that *she* was a possible suspect in the fire, her fantasies about moving all her shoes into Jenny's closet were replaced by nightmares of living at home and being forced to go to Atlanta public school with a bunch of kooky rednecks.

"Thanks for meeting me. You know CoffeeRoasters and Maxwell's were far too public." Tinsley took a sip of her cappuccino. Her thick black hair was swept up in a sloppy bun and secured by a pair of turquoise lacquered chopsticks, and she wore a navy Wayne sailor minidress that hugged her in all the right places. On anyone else, the outfit would have looked like a slutty Halloween costume, but Tinsley looked beautiful, as always.

What was amazing was how unthreatened Callie felt about her perfect-looking best friend these days. Despite the pimple threatening to break out above her left eye, and the two pounds she'd certainly put on over the weekend, drinking beer and eating anything Easy offered her, she felt more secure and confident than ever. She and Easy were in love again, even more so than before, and they had actually done it. It was incredible. She felt so . . . adult. *Take that, Carmichael*.

"Maybe I should've worn my Ella Moss wrap dress—you know that one that always looks like it's going to unwrap? It worked on Dalton." Tinsley leaned back in the booth and smiled fondly at the ancient tin ceiling. "Actually, it works on everyone. I still can't believe Marymount didn't believe me."

Callie sipped her cappuccino slowly.

"Anyway." Tinsley leaned in. "I'm not too worried about it." She waved her hand as if swatting away an annoying fly. Her silver Anaconda ring sparkled in the morning light. "It isn't going to be *us* that gets sent home, that much I can guarantee you."

The thought of moving back into her bedroom at home in Atlanta, in the enormous stone governor's mansion on Paces Ferry Road, with its pale pink rug and creepy canopy bed, gave Callie the shivers. So did the thought of having breakfast every morning with her overly coiffed mother. "How can you be sure?" Callie asked worriedly. She pressed her palms against the sides of her cup, enjoying the feel of heat seeping through her skin. "Marymount must have something on all of us if he's calling us suspects."

"Could be a bluff," Tinsley suggested confidently, smoothing a stray wisp of hair behind her left ear. "I've seen it a million times before."

Callie tried not to roll her hazel eyes. Just because Tinsley's passport had been stamped by just about every country in the world, she acted like she was so much more worldly and wise than everyone else. Callie had a feeling that was why Tinsley hadn't pressed her for details about what was going on with Easy—she didn't really want to know. It had recently come to light in a game of I Never that Tinsley was a virgin, and Callie was sure she couldn't stand the idea that Callie had done something that she hadn't. "Oh, yeah? Like, where?"

Tinsley narrowed her violet-colored eyes at her friend, her lips twitching at Callie's challenge. "The movies."

Callie snickered, licked her pointer finger, and stuck it in the lumpy raw sugar granules she'd spilled on her saucer.

Tinsley watched her. "That's really gross, you know." She removed the chopsticks from her dark hair and shook it out so it fell in waves over her shoulders. She raised her perfectly plucked left eyebrow, waiting for Callie to stop.

"But this isn't a movie." Callie felt the hint of a whine starting to creep into her voice. If Tinsley got kicked out of school, what would happen? Nothing. She'd go to South fucking Africa with her dad and make an award-winning documentary and get to meet George Clooney and Brad Pitt and all the other do-gooder A-listers at Cannes and Sundance. Oh, wait. She'd pretty much already done that. Only Tinsley could get kicked out of Waverly for doing E and come back smelling like roses. "You know my mother will sentence me to death if I get kicked out, right?" She wasn't even sure if Georgia had the death penalty, but even if it didn't, her mom would sign it into law.

Tinsley stared over Callie's shoulder at the picture of downtown Rhinecliff from the 1920s—it looked about as exciting as it did today. "If it *was* a movie, who would play you?"

"Grace Kelly," Callie answered immediately, holding her head up in what she probably thought was a princess-of-Monaco-worthy pose. She straightened the neck on her Joie silk ruffle top and looked out the window, staring out at the clear blue sky. Her eyes were distant. "The thing is, the list seems so *random*. Why is someone like Brandon Buchanan on it and not a freaking pothead like Alan St. Girard?"

Tinsley gulped her cooling cappuccino. She knew why Callie was on the list, and Easy—because she herself had blurted to the dean that they were in the barn. Not that she'd told Callie as much. She knew why Jenny and Julian were on the list, too. And of course, she knew why *she* was on the list. She was still mad at herself for fumbling her meeting with the dean.

"I wish I had come with you to Dean Marymount's office," Callie sighed, as if reading her mind. She twirled one of her strawberry blond locks nervously with the same finger she'd been sticking in the sugar. She was probably getting grains of sugar in her hair. Maybe Easy would like that.

"I wish you had, too." Tinsley narrowed her eyes. She hoped she had achieved the right degree of chastisement in her tone. It served Callie right for ditching her. The disastrous scene in the dean's office replayed in her head. Maybe if she hadn't been so focused on Marymount's gross unibrow, or her bizarre image of him as a hawk eating his students, or his sad family picture . . .

"Oh my God." She sat up straighter in the booth. Callie looked at her in confusion, and Tinsley grinned, feeling positively gleeful. "I've got it!"

"So, Chloe." Tinsley swirled her chocolate milk shake with a straw. "How are you enjoying Waverly so far?"

A tray of glasses shattered against the floor and everyone in Nocturne, the newly opened twenty-four-hour diner on the far end of Main Street in Rhinecliff, turned to look. Everyone except Tinsley, whose eyes were locked on the young prospective as though the girl held the key to salvation. Tinsley had picked a good spot for covert business, Callie thought. Nocturne was so new that it wasn't yet on the faculty's radar, and she was sure the retro, '50s-style diner would be filled tonight with Owls eating grilled cheese and curly fries after curfew. Callie watched as the red-faced waitress swept up shards of glass that shone like diamonds against the diner's black-and-white-checkered floor.

"It's been okay," Chloe replied tentatively. She was probably still a little shocked that Tinsley Carmichael had invited her to lunch off campus. Tinsley had lured her here on the premise of "getting to know her," but as always with Tinsley, there was an ulterior motive. She had figured out where she recognized Chloe from: Dean Marymount's family picture. The little twerp was his *niece*, and, as Tinsley's scheming mind quickly discerned, she'd been feeding him information. Most likely, the dean's list of "suspects" was nothing more than all the people who had been rude to Chloe over the weekend. Not that they were the most innocent people or anything, but still. That didn't make them *arsonists*.

"The thing to keep in mind is that you're seeing the school at a very unique time," Tinsley noted as she stabbed a leaf of her Caesar salad. "We're all just so *stressed* about the fire." Tinsley put down her fork, as if the stress had ruined her appetite, and leaned back against the red vinyl cushions of the booth. Her perfect brow was wrinkled in worry.

Callie took a big bite of her burger, not sure if she could keep a straight face as she watched Tinsley's dramatics. Ever since she and Easy had gotten back together, she'd been ravenous—probably because of all the calories they were burning.

Chloe picked at her tuna melt and Tater Tots. "It's totally crazy," she agreed. "But it will all be over soon, won't it?" She looked back and forth between the two older girls questioningly. Callie narrowed her eyes at the prospective, wondering how much of her apparent innocence was an act. With her shoulder-length pale blond hair and pale skin, and wearing a pale yellow cable-knit sweater, she looked like a giant, undercooked french fry.

"Hopefully," Callie piped up, setting her burger down. She grabbed a napkin from the chrome holder and wiped her mouth. She fought the urge to ask the waitress for a bib—the last thing she wanted to do was spill on her new ruffly lavender Joie top. "*If* they catch the right person. But from what I can tell, they're not going to."

"Really?" Chloe asked, looking up at Callie. She rolled the sleeves up on her sweater. "Why do you say that?"

Tinsley pulled the long silver spoon from her tall glass of frothy milk shake, licked it clean, and pointed it right between Chloe's eyes. "Because the real culprit is doe-eyed and innocent-looking, just like you," she replied matter-of-factly. She placed the spoon down on the Formica countertop. "You may have met her, actually. Her name is Jenny Humphrey."

Callie scanned the restaurant, hoping no one from Waverly was within earshot. Either nobody had wanted to venture off campus for lunch, or Nocturne was even newer than she'd realized, because she didn't recognize a single face. Besides, the jukebox was playing a selection of cheesy '50s songs nonstop—"My Boyfriend's Back" was currently blaring through the speakers— so she doubted anyone at the next booth could even hear them.

Chloe's baby blue eyes widened. "Jenny? I met her. She goes out with Julian, right? He's so cute."

Tinsley flinched. It was bad enough that Heath knew about her and Julian and was sending her snide IMs throwing it in her face. Now she had to listen to this little prospective talk about the freakishly hot freshman and his gigantic-boobed girlfriend. If she heard Jenny and Julian mentioned in the same breath again, she was going to throw her milk shake clear across the diner. And if she ever *saw* them together again, she just might start another fire—this time intentionally. Wednesday's meeting, and Jenny Humphrey's expulsion from Waverly, could not come quickly enough.

"Did she really start the fire?" Chloe continued, her high-pitched voice sounding almost like a whine.

"Yes." Callie nodded definitively, turning to the younger girl. "I *saw* her with a lighter in her hand, by the barn. But I can't tell the administration that, because then *I'll* seem suspicious for having been there. Can you imagine how terrible it feels, to know someone's guilty but not to be able to tell the truth?" She sighed dramatically and slumped against the red vinyl of the diner's booth.

Chloe looked like a Tater Tot might have lodged in her esophagus. "But," she sputtered, "she could be dangerous!" Behind her glasses, her blue eyes looked truly frightened.

"You're exactly right." Tinsley leaned forward conspiratorially, pushing her salad aside. She locked her violet eyes on Chloe's. "Which is why we have to be vigilant, and really watch her today and tomorrow. With the list of suspects released, she's probably feeling backed against a wall, and who knows what she could do?" Tinsley leaned back in the booth again, patted her neat black ponytail, and straightened her sailor dress. "So maybe we should make a pact that we'll all keep an eye on Jenny? And that if we see anything suspicious, we'll make sure to tell each other?"

Chloe put down her tuna melt excitedly. "You want *me* to help?"

"Of course." Tinsley nodded briskly. She lowered her voice to a whisper, as if she were entrusting Chloe with CIA secrets. "We *need* you to help."

Chloe wiped her hand on a napkin. She took her glasses off, and her eyes, which looked even more enormous without glasses, darted between Callie and Tinsley. "Okay," she said slowly. "But if I help and, um, keep an eye on Jenny, what's in it for me?"

"Well," Tinsley said sweetly, a familiar glint in her eye, "let's just say that when you start Waverly next fall, you'll have the two most popular senior girls for best friends." The jukebox changed to Elvis's "Don't Be Cruel," and Tinsley smiled her patented Carmichael smile, the one that seemed to say, *I'm holding all the cards, but be honored that I've let you play.*

Chloe straightened in the booth, as if aware of the new responsibility that had been laid upon her shoulders. "That sounds cool." She nodded, putting her glasses back on and pushing them up against the bridge of her nose. "I've always wanted to be popular."

Callie shook her head and took a sip of Diet Coke. Of course she did—who didn't? Callie had learned quickly at Waverly never to underestimate the strength of a girl's—any girl's—ambitions.

OwlNet

BennyCunningham: So, you coming to the crater tomorrow?

LonBaruzza: To see you off? Wouldn't miss it for the world.

BennyCunningham: Good. Bet you'd be fun to order around.

LonBaruzza: Oh, just try me.

BennyCunningham: How are you at back rubs?

LonBaruzza: Incomparable.

BrandonBuchanan: What do you know about Sage Francis?

RyanReynolds: Why u asking?

BrandonBuchanan: Just answer the question.

RyanReynolds: Well, she's single . . . and she's HAWT.

BrandonBuchanan: Thanks, that's all I needed to know.

RyanReynolds: Only trouble is, she's hottie for my body. So don't go there.

BrandonBuchanan: Reynolds, nobody is hottie for your anything. Get ahold of yourself. No one else will.

HeathFerro: Do you have a size small dress shirt?

KaraWhalen: What?

HeathFerro: Come on. Help a Woman of Waverly in need.
                  It's not like I'm asking to borrow your panties.
                  Tho now that I think about it . . .

KaraWhalen: You're a nut. Come on over.

A RESPONSIBLE OWL KNOWS BETTER THAN TO
PESTER THE DEAN'S SECRETARY.

Brett's face fell when she saw Mr. Tomkins's bald dome of a head hunched in front of his flat-screen monitor, blocking her path to Marymount's office. She'd decided to come at lunchtime, when Mr. Tomkins was usually in the dining hall, loading up on beets, asparagus, and chicken breast at the salad bar. She bet his pee smelled like dead cat.

Brett knew something was afoot as soon as Mr. Tomkins looked up from his desk at her and put down his tuna on rye. He straightened his black tie with tiny jack-o'-lanterns all over it. Wasn't it a little early for Halloween? She shuddered at the idea of him dressed up in the same Headless Horseman costume as last year, which had involved a weird leather hood that looked like it had come from a sex shop. It was actually really scary, especially when she tried not to think about what he did with the costume the rest of the year in the privacy of his own home. The legend of Sleepy Hollow had taken on a whole new, totally pornographic meaning.

"Is he in?" Brett asked, tilting her head to the side so that her fire engine red hair fell like a curtain to her shoulder. In her red-and-black-plaid wool James Perse jumper, worn over a flirty white hippie shirt she'd borrowed from Kara last week, Brett hoped she looked appropriately innocent.

Mr. Tomkins nodded slowly, wiping his lips with a scrunched-up napkin. "That he is." He'd evidently given up pretending he had any hair left and had gone ahead and shaved the last ten hairs completely off. Brett moved toward Marymount's closed door and Mr. Tomkins flinched. His whole body tensed up, as if he were ready to spring out of his chair and throw himself in front of the door if necessary. "But he can't be disturbed."

Disturbed? Since when was a visit from the junior class prefect a disruption? And since when was Mr. Tomkins, who adored Brett, acting all secrety? "Why not?" she demanded, instantly aware of the fact that she should be buttering Tomkins up instead of challenging him. But it was an urgent situation, and Brett was too annoyed, and a little scared, at being named a suspect to waste her time flirting with Mr. Tomkins. She always suspected he just acted effeminate so that the girls would be less self-conscious about bending over or adjusting their bra straps in front of him. Perv.

"He's busy preparing his speech for the prospective-student welcome dinner tonight," Mr. Tomkins informed her. She noticed a tiny splotch of mustard on his tie and knew he'd be mortified when he found it. "He left strict instructions not to be disturbed."

"But it's an *emergency*." Brett felt her ten-year-old whine creeping into her voice and swallowed hard. She wasn't going to beg Mr. Tomkins. It was humiliating enough having her name associated with the fire—why the hell was she on the list, anyway? "And I'm the junior class prefect," Brett added desperately, knowing that she was getting on Mr. Tomkins's nerves. She wondered if she should just compliment him on his shaved skull and be done with it. "I'm here on school business."

Mr. Tomkins stared at her, leaning back in his antique oak chair. "What business is that?"

"You know." Brett felt herself grasping for words. So much for two years on the debate team, preparing herself for confrontation. She placed her palms on the bare surface of Mr. Tomkins's polished oak desk and smiled pleadingly at him. "I just need to speak with him for a minute. Can't you get me in for one minute? You can time me."

Mr. Tomkins smiled, amused, and shook his head no. Brett heard a rustling behind the dean's door and waited with anticipation for it to open, but the rustling died down and the office grew quiet again.

"He simply can't be disturbed," Mr. Tomkins repeated, half looking at his computer screen, one hand perched on the mouse. *Easy job*, Brett thought bitterly. Eating tuna sandwiches at your desk and surfing the Web for Sleepy Hollow porn all day, throwing out a student here and there. "I wish I could help you."

"I'm a prefect—" Brett ramped up for a second go-round with that approach.

"Yes, I'm aware of that," Mr. Tomkins interrupted. He didn't look up from his screen this time, and Brett had the feeling that he was completely absorbed in a game of solitaire.

"—and I have a right to know why I'm a suspect." Brett blushed, a little worried about being overhead dealing in her own self-interest, especially after having pretended to represent the student body as a whole. But there wasn't anyone else in the office, and if the dean heard her, well, maybe then he'd let her in.

"I'm sorry." Mr. Tomkins sounded about as unsorry as possible. "I can't divulge that information." He had a self-satisfied, I-know-something-you-don't-know smile on his face, and Brett didn't want to give him the satisfaction of begging him to "divulge" that "information." She was about to turn and leave when Mr. Tomkins surprised her by lowering his voice to a whisper. "But I imagine *some* students are on the list because they haven't exactly kept a low profile as of late."

For half a second, she thought he must have meant Heath. Or Tinsley. Or even Jenny, who seemed to be the subject of a million conversations, along with Easy and Callie.

But as she looked at his pointedly raised eyebrows, she realized that Mr. Tomkins meant *her*. Her stomach plummeted to the toes of her red suede Campers. *You have got to be kidding me!* Brett wanted to scream at Tomkins, who was pretending not to notice the look of horror on her face. *I'm on the list because I don't lock myself in my room and study all the time? I'm on the list because my classmates have been gossiping about me? I'm on the list because I kissed another girl?* How was that even *possible?* Horrified, her knees shaking, Brett stumbled out of the office, not even bothering to say goodbye.

Out in the hall, she collapsed on the hard wooden bench, where countless numbers of delinquents had been forced to wait while Marymount arbitrarily decided their fate. She imagined Dean Marymount and Mr. Tomkins and a flock of other nosy teachers, gleefully huddled around a Waverly yearbook, pointing their fingers and cheering when they found someone who looked appropriately guilty. She could just see their faces when they reached her picture. Mr. Tomkins would pull on his jack-o'-lantern tie.

"Hmmm, yes." Dean Marymount would pet his thin sandy comb-over. "Sketchy lesbian pyro. Even if she is the junior class prefect, better put her on the list." Then he'd nod sagely before writing down her name, in permanent ink, with the word *guilty* underlined next to it.

KaraWhalen: Want to head over to the prospectives' dinner together later?

BrettMesserschmidt: I might just order in instead. . . .

KaraWhalen: How come?

BrettMesserschmidt: Yeah, I sort of feel like lying low.

KaraWhalen: Hey, there's nothing to worry about. We're on the dean's list, but we didn't do anything wrong, right?

BrettMesserschmidt: Depends on who you ask.

A WAVERLY OWL NEVER FORFEITS A MATCH.

Tinsley made her way down the gravelly path to Dumbarton, her white leather Prince tennis shoes cushioning each step. Practice today had been more amusing than usual. Ms. Nemerov, the ultra-fit, slightly mannish Russian coach, was unabashedly giving Tinsley special treatment due to the dean's list of suspects—she was horror-struck at the idea that her star player could be taken away, and had even brought Tinsley aside and offered to put in a good word for her to Dean Marymount. Tinsley politely declined. She was doing just fine on her own, thank you very much. With Chloe's help, the dean would already be convinced Jenny was the culprit by Wednesday's meeting. Tinsley felt like a puppeteer playing with her marionettes, holding all the strings.

On the lawn, a flock of underclass girls in tank tops were sprawled out on a maroon Waverly stadium blanket, their

skinny arms soaking up the last gasps of the summer sun-
shine before it was gone completely. They all turned, almost
imperceptibly, from the books they were pretending to study
to watch Tinsley, and she had to stifle a smile. She sliced her
racket through the air as she walked, imagining Jenny's head
on the chopping block. She didn't notice the tall, lanky figure
approaching her until she'd nearly run into him.

"Tinsley," Julian announced abruptly, and she almost
jumped.

"Julian," she replied automatically, unable to think of anything else to say. Faced with his adorable rangy figure and his
puppy-dog brown eyes, she felt strangely nervous. Her stomach
flip-flopped as she remembered their sexy encounters all over
campus—the Dumbarton bathroom, the movie screening room
in the basement of Hopkins Hall. She'd turned it into a top
secret affair, all because she was afraid of the world finding out
she liked a freshman. But really, now that she thought about it,
how bad could it have been? She probably would have started a
trend, à la Demi Moore.

"Hey, I'm, uh, sorry we never really talked this weekend."
Julian dug a toe into the gravel path. He looked up again, his
shaggy blond-brown hair falling messily across his forehead.
He wore a yellow plaid button-down, and Tinsley wondered
what he had on underneath. "Things just got sort of crazy. But
I really did want to talk to you about some stuff."

Tinsley straightened, feeling like she'd just been slapped
in the face. She chastised herself for her moment of weakness.
Why did she let this freshman get under her skin? "Some *stuff?*"

she asked icily, narrowing her violet eyes. "And by 'things got sort of crazy,' you mean you were too busy with your new girl-friend?"

"What are you talking about?" Julian looked genuinely confused. He ran a hand through his messy hair, probably won-dering how she knew about Jenny. Did he really think he could sneak around with that top-heavy little slutbag without her finding out?

"Don't play dumb with me. I *saw* you with that midget." She rested her titanium tennis racket on the ground and leaned on it, feeling like she'd just won match point.

Julian raised his eyebrows. She couldn't tell if he was sur-prised or angry. Probably both. "When?"

Tinsley froze, realizing her mistake. If she told him she'd seen them outside the barn, she'd practically be admitting to arson. She stole a glance to her left. The sunbathing girls were still engrossed in their books, though she suspected they were straining to hear every word of her conversation. "It doesn't matter when," she hissed. "But I'll make this easy for you. The next time I see you and your little girlfriend together might be your *last time together*." She said the last words slowly and care-fully. She didn't want to have to repeat herself.

Julian's face turned slightly pink. "Are you threatening me?" His voice wavered and he lost his usual easy composure, seeming both shocked and a little scared. Which was exactly how Tinsley wanted her opponents to feel.

"Don't be silly," she laughed, tossing her black, silky hair. "I think we both know who I'm threatening."

She turned on her heel and walked off, swinging her racket daintily. Game, set, match. But the loser here wasn't Julian. It was someone much, much shorter.

For the special dinner that night to honor the prospectives, the dining hall had apparently been transformed from a mundane eating establishment into a five-star restaurant. The setting sun glinted through the stained glass windows, sending sprays of color across the white linen tablecloths. Irritated as she was at the presence of all the geeky prospectives—well, all but one— Tinsley was impressed that Marymount had splurged like this for their benefit. She paused in the doorway, both to admire the changes and to allow everyone the opportunity to see that she was as calm and unperturbed as ever, despite Marymount's threatening e-mail.

Gone were the pizza bar and the cereal bins—even the soda fountains had been pushed back and turned toward the wall, replaced by a dizzying array of servers clad in pressed white shirts, black pants, and white gloves. Tinsley nearly knocked over one carrying a tray of canapés. Hors d'oeuvre trays? Apparently, when it came to securing Waverly's financial future, the dean was more than willing to open his wallet a little. Someone had even gone to the trouble of calligraphing a sign stating ABSOLUTELY NO CELL PHONES, displayed prominently at the entrance.

She was one of the last to arrive, but she preferred it that way. She felt everyone's eyes on her as she strode across the dining room in her vintage black Chanel baby doll dress and dark patterned stockings, walking in a way that made the somewhat shapeless dress come to life and cause everyone to wonder about the body underneath.

One of the long tables near the giant stone fireplace—in which a heap of logs had been set ablaze for the occasion, Tinsley noted with irony—had been overtaken by Sage and Benny and company. "Nice dress, T," Benny offered up in a loud whisper as Tinsley passed.

"Thanks," Tinsley answered in her regular voice, which made her realize how silent the cavernous dining hall was. Heads were pressed together at every table, and low whispering filled the air, as if everyone was afraid that speaking out loud would somehow indicate their guilt. At the other end of the table Callie caught Tinsley's eye. She leaned her strawberry blond head toward Easy, who was practically sitting on top of her. *Get a room,* Tinsley snickered to herself. Callie beckoned her over with a raised blond eyebrow, patting the seat next to her with her Swarovski-pearl-braceleted hand.

Tinsley squeezed past the other Owls toward Callie's end of the table, where Heath was trying to convince one of the servers to set her tray of hors d'oeuvres down directly in front of him. Whispering erupted in Tinsley's wake, and she smiled to herself. She didn't mind being named a suspect in the Miller fire—anyone who'd read any Agatha Christie knew that the culprit was always the person least expected. Someone, for example, like little Jenny Humphrey. No one could imagine her sweet little five-foot self setting a barn on fire, but when she finally got busted for doing it, everyone would wonder why they hadn't realized it sooner.

"Nice entrance," Callie hissed under her breath. "Mary-mount's supposed to speak in like two minutes."

Tinsley slid into the uncomfortable oak chair Callie had reserved for her. "Well, it's not like he'd start without me," she whispered back with a smirk.

Brandon Buchanan was trying to surreptitiously pass a note scrawled on a napkin to someone at the other end of the table. Reflexively, Tinsley intercepted it and held it in her hand. Brandon, in a neatly ironed Armani dress shirt and tie, smirked at her, daring her to open it. She uncrumpled the napkin. *Think she did it?* it read in Brandon's surprisingly sloppy cursive. Tinsley stuck her tongue out at Brandon—was he talking about her? She definitely wouldn't mind too much if that know-it-all got kicked out—and crumpled up the napkin. All of the tables had little clusters of crumpled napkins scattered around, and Tinsley wondered how many others contained notes about her.

"T.C." Heath nodded a formal hello as one of the servers—a cute blond sophomore—parked an entire tray of stuffed mushrooms in front of him.

Tinsley just stared back. She hadn't noticed the prospective sitting next to Heath before. His light brown hair was gelled into place exactly the same way as Heath's—sides back, top tousled artistically and frozen into place—and Tinsley did a double take, wondering if Heath had a little brother. As the kid reached for a stuffed mushroom, she noticed that he even kind of *moved* like Heath. Freaky. He plopped the mushroom into his mouth, not stopping to roll up the cinched sleeve on his baby blue dress shirt. It looked like it had come from the Junior Miss section of Bloomingdale's.

"I like your shirt," Tinsley noted, forgetting to whisper. The entire table turned in alarm, as if they were hiding from the enemy and she had given away their position.

"Yeah, it's cool," the prospective said, mimicking Heath's head bob as he spoke.

"That's my boy, Sam," Heath whispered, making little fists of triumph with his hands. Sam immediately imitated the gesture, and everyone at the table snickered.

"I didn't know you were a father, Ferro." Alan St. Girard leaned forward, snatching up one of Heath's mushrooms. He'd shaved his beard scruff for the occasion, revealing the baby fat on his pinkish cheeks. Tinsley glanced around to see where his girlfriend was and spotted Alison Quentin's glossy black head at a round table in the corner of the room, where she was sitting with Jenny and, she noted with pleasure, Chloe. Taking a sip of water, she scanned the room, finally spotting Julian's familiar handsome head at a table of squash players tucked in the corner, about as far from Jenny's table as possible. She took another sip of water, pretending it was champagne, and congratulated herself on a job well done.

"He's my protégé," Heath boasted, patting Sam on the shoulder. "He's going to carry on the Ferro legacy long after I'm gone."

"Which could be soon, right?" Tinsley smiled, leaning back in her chair and crossing her arms in front of her, which she knew drew attention to her perfect chest.

"We'll see," Heath said, glancing around.

A murmur spread through the room as Dean Marymount ascended the podium, decorated with the Waverly crest, at the front of the dining hall. He surveyed the crowd and said something no one could hear, reaching under the podium to turn on the microphone. Everyone glanced around at each other, but the room remained surprisingly silent. He tapped the microphone with two thick fingers and a sound like staticky thunder echoed in everyone's ears. Finally, a few snickers spread through the crowd. Tinsley kept a straight face, not even looking away when Marymount seemed to rest his eyes directly on her.

"We're very pleased to welcome our visitors," he began, his voice grave and serious, as if he were addressing the Supreme Court and not a group of rowdy teenagers. "Tradition is an important part of Waverly's continued reputation for excellence. Our standing not just in the immediate community but in the community at large is a worthy combination of honor and respect, which are two-way streets, intersected by a wide boulevard known as truth."

Tinsley pressed her lips together and stared at Marymount, cupping her chin in her palm in what she hoped looked like a gesture of interest. She stared at the last stuffed mushroom on Heath's plate, her stomach letting out a tiny growl. "Respect for each other and for our community is central to what makes Waverly an honorable institution. Do not forget that Waverly is not just a place. It has a character and a moral fiber of its own, and each and every person who dons a Waverly blazer and takes on the proud title of Waverly Owl becomes part of the

fabric of our community. If we want the school to be honorable, we must be honorable individuals. An Owl is, above all,
moral, principled, and an upright citizen. These are the qualities every Waverly student should embody, a truth I hope the
prospectives—our future Waverly Owls—will intuit from you
this weekend as you continue to inspire their quest to join the
Waverly community." Marymount paused dramatically, drawing in his breath and making sure he had everyone's attention
before he delivered his next line: "Of course, it goes without
saying that anyone who doesn't embody the qualities we cherish
dearly at Waverly does not belong here, and can only become
a blemish on Waverly's long-standing, hard-earned reputation.
Rest assured that Waverly will not suffer any embarrassments
on my watch. That much I promise you."

Marymount looked up from the podium, his cold blue eyes
searching the crowd like a hawk. Tinsley glanced around at her
classmates. Everyone around her had averted his or her eyes,
seemingly afraid to make eye contact with the dean. The only
person oblivious to the dean's ominous message was Sam, who
had just discovered that the buttons on his shirt were a pearly
pink and not white. He stared down at them in dismay. Tinsley
wondered how he'd overlooked the Peter Pan collar and pleated
shoulders.

She glanced again in Jenny's direction. She hung on Marymount's every word, looking worried, her dark curls less perky
than usual. Next to her, Chloe turned and caught Tinsley's eye.
The prospective gave her a super-obvious wink, looking like
she was trying very hard not to wave and shout, "I'm friends

with Tinsley!" She might not have been all that suave, but she was invaluable.

Tinsley smiled. Dean Marymount didn't realize—at least, not yet—that the person he was describing to a T was, in fact, little Jenny Humphrey. How could anyone with a chest like that have morals?

From: RufusHumphrey@poetsonline.com
To: JenniferHumphrey@waverly.edu
Date: Monday, October 14, 10:27 P.M.
Subject: Meow!

Meow Mrowr (Dear Jenny),

Everyone here at West 99th Street and West End Ave misses you, especially me, Marx the Cat. Rotting milk doesn't taste the same when you're not around, and I can barely muster the energy to chase mice onto the fire escape. I've taken to sleeping in your old bed, but the girl who sleeps there now, the one that doesn't have any hair—what breed is she, a Sphinx?—doesn't seem too happy about that. Probably because she only wears black, a color that shows up fur very nicely.

Dearest Jenny, my favorite owner, when will we be seeing you again? Your absence is as tough to swallow as a very large furball.

Sincerely,

Marx the Cat

P.S. Please call your father! He seems lonely without you. He won't stop brushing me.

THE WAVERLY LIBRARY IS A PLACE FOR
SERIOUS STUDY.

Tuesday morning, Callie caught a whiff of oil paint in the air as she turned the corner on the second floor of the library, her Costume National heels clicking. She glanced at her slim Cartier bracelet-watch with tiny diamonds circling the face and smiled to herself. Right on time. It was her first trip to the Staxxx, a superprivate nook of the library reserved for those studying for the SATs and known for its lack of surveillance by the roving librarians. The books on the corner shelves were mostly old encyclopedias and obsolete reference books, so no one ever wandered there accidentally. Some enterprising student had started a private library on the lower shelf of the Staxxx: tattered copies of *Lady Chatterley's Lover*, *Lolita*, a Henry Miller omnibus of *Sexus*, *Nexus*, and *Plexus*. And of course there was the issue of *Playboy* featuring nude photos of Madonna taped underneath the far bookshelf, courtesy of the Waverly Class of 1985.

She found Easy sitting in one of the three diner-like study booths, the seats cushioned in itchy orange plaid wool. The idea behind the booths had been to encourage group studying, but mostly it was work of the one-on-one nature that got done in them instead.

"Hey." Easy's deep blue eyes lit up when he saw her. He tossed aside his copy of *Tropic of Cancer*. In his black waffle-knit tee and destroyed Levi's, with his dark curls slightly matted across his forehead, he looked positively edible.

Callie let her black leather Pierre Hardy saddle bag drop to the floor and immediately threw herself into the side of the booth where Easy was sitting, tackling him roughly.

"Oof!" Easy's knee banged against the edge of the table. He grinned slowly, a small crust of white toothpaste stuck in the corner of his mouth. Callie licked her finger and painted the toothpaste away. "Thanks, Mom," he drawled, and Callie smacked him lightly on the shoulder before scooting off him. She traced her fingers down his leg, loving how square and boy-like his giant knees were beneath their super-soft denim. She couldn't tear her gaze from his beautiful blue eyes. They reminded Callie of the ocean, but not the bright, Caribbean turquoise one that everyone loved to snorkel in—the dark, out-in-the-middle-of-the-Atlantic Ocean, whose depths you couldn't even fathom.

Easy leaned forward and kissed her on the lips. It started out sweet and tender, and then slowly, it began to build and build, until they both had to pull away. They stared at each other, knowing exactly what the other was thinking.

"Want me to, uh, put *Lolita* on the book cart by the door?" Easy asked in a low voice, referring to the time-honored signal that the Staxxx were in use. His Kentucky accent became more pronounced the more turned on he got, and right now, Callie could barely tell he'd spent the last two and half years at an East Coast prep school. His finger ran around the top of her Habitual stovepipe jeans, brushing lightly against the small of her back. Callie felt her stomach drop, the way it did in the high-speed elevator that took her to her father's office at the top of the Bank of America skyscraper in downtown Atlanta.

"What if we get caught?" she asked, only half concerned. The library was always dead in the morning, and besides, everyone was too busy stressing about the barn investigation to even think about having an SAT study party. She slipped off her eggplant TSE cardigan, revealing a thin white Anthropologie camisole underneath.

"Who cares?" Easy shrugged. "It might be our last chance. We ought to jump at every opportunity." He had meant it as a joke, but as soon as the words left his lips, Easy felt his stomach flip-flop. Ever since the dean's e-mail he'd been a nervous wreck, and he'd hardly slept at all last night. He'd been in trouble many, many times at Waverly, and even though he'd heard about that kid Julian's lighter being found, he somehow felt that the accusatory e-mail had been directed at him, and him alone. He wouldn't be surprised if within the week he'd been kicked out of Waverly, disinherited by his father, and sent to reform school. He wasn't so much afraid for himself as for Callie. What would she do if he got kicked out? And what would he do if *she* got kicked out?

"Don't be silly." Callie shook her head, her wavy blond hair brushing her bare shoulders. "We're not going anywhere."

Easy put his hand behind Callie's neck, loving the feel of her bare, soft skin. "It was a joke, but . . . babe, Marymount's looking to kick someone out. And we were in the barn. We're probably his number-one suspects." He slid his hand down to Callie's shoulder. "How come you're not worried?" It struck him that he was acting all paranoid and, well, Callie-like, and she was acting all mellow and Easy-like. How had that happened? Did she know something he didn't?

Callie shrugged, her hazel eyes seeming unconcerned. "I just have faith that whoever's responsible will be punished." She leaned in to nuzzle his neck. "You need to relax," she whispered in a low, throaty voice.

But he couldn't relax. Callie had told him the morning after the fire that she was positive Jenny had started it out of jealousy. Which meant that when she said "*whoever* was responsible," she really meant Jenny. And what was that hushed phone call with Tinsley about in the stables the other day? It was weird that Callie and Tinsley were suddenly all chummy again. Easy sat up suddenly. "You're not up to anything, are you?" he asked. His words hung in the air, and he worried that he was just being paranoid, but it was too late.

Callie blinked her eyes slowly. Her lashes were blond and pretty without the black gunk she had on them half the time.

"Of course not." She tossed her head, her strawberry blond hair falling messily into place. She'd cut off her long locks a few weeks ago, and now they fell right around her shoulders, framing her long, thin neck. "I just meant that we're innocent and don't have anything to worry about." She leaned forward again and nibbled on his earlobe, her hot breath in his ear. "Now where were we?"

Easy closed his eyes. Being with Callie felt so good. He didn't want their relationship tainted by his paranoia about Dean Marymount's suspect list and the fire. If she said there was nothing going on, there was nothing going on. "We were right here," he whispered back, and kissed her soft, pillowy lips. Callie had said it from the beginning: They were together again, and that was all that mattered.

CallieVernon:	I can't go through with this.
TinsleyCarmichael:	Huh?
CallieVernon:	EZ suspects I'm up to something.
TinsleyCarmichael:	And?
CallieVernon:	And . . . I can't risk it. Can you take it from here?
TinsleyCarmichael:	Jesus. Grow some, C.
CallieVernon:	Don't be like that. You know you've got cojones for both of us.

14

A WAVERLY OWL KNOWS A PICTURE IS WORTH

A THOUSAND WORDS.

Normally Jenny loved the buzzing sounds of her favorite art class, portraiture. The stools scraping across the concrete floor and paintbrushes scratching across canvas were usually enough to inspire her to get to work. Once the scent of oil and turpentine hit the air, she couldn't have stopped if she wanted to.

But today, her fingers felt heavy and sluggish. Even with her purple ArtBin spread open in front of her, and all her Derwent drawing pencils lined up according to hardness, her hands were rigid with worry. She stared at the blank white drawing paper. Mrs. Silver had instructed them at the beginning of class to draw or paint whatever they liked, so long as it "tapped into their innermost thoughts and feelings." It was sort of a hippie-dippy exercise, but everyone seemed excited to get a break from all the strict rules they faced elsewhere. While all the other students were busy sketching or painting, Jenny had frozen up. It was as though she'd been trying so hard to suppress her innermost thoughts and feelings that now she couldn't access them, like a faucet that had gone dry from lack of use.

Mrs. Silver suddenly loomed over Jenny's shoulder, her round, friendly Mrs. Claus–like face screwed up in a question mark. Today she wore a purple-sea-horse-batiked minidress with sparkly silver leggings and dark brown Ugg boots.

"Trouble getting started?" she asked, plopping a doughy hand down on Jenny's shoulder. Jenny nodded slowly.

"Put the pencil down," Mrs. Silver instructed her. Jenny slipped the charcoal pencil back in the tray, in its correct spot between 2B and 4B. When had she become so anal? "Now. Take a deep breath." She inhaled and exhaled quietly, hoping no one around her would think she was about to have a seizure or something.

"No, no, no," Mrs. Silver clucked. Her frizzy gray hair was pulled back into two messy buns near the back of her head, but new wisps escaped each time she moved. The sea horses on her minidress danced. "That wasn't deep enough. Try again."

Jenny glanced around, feeling self-conscious as she inhaled deeply, filling up every single inch of her lungs with turpentine-fumed air. She felt her chest expand—not something she really needed—but soon she felt little tingles of life start to spring into her arms and hands and then her whole body. She exhaled loudly, not caring if anyone was watching.

"Much, much better." Mrs. Silver giggled happily and clamped her hands on her full hips, lowering her voice so that

Jenny had to lean toward her to hear the words. "I want you to communicate with your subconscious. The purpose of this exercise is to let go, to just draw without constraint." Her hands flitted about, making phantom drawings in the air. "Don't worry about what it's going to be—maybe when you're done, it won't look like *anything*. I just want you to put pencil to paper and see what happens."

Jenny nodded again. She was having trouble reining in her thoughts, which were mostly preoccupied with Dean Marymount's veiled threat at the welcome dinner last night. And then there was the upcoming Usual Suspects party. At first, Jenny hadn't been going to go. Watching Callie and Easy celebrate their possible last night together didn't exactly make her want to party. But ever since the dean's e-mail had circulated, Jenny had been feeling isolated. She wondered if the other Usual Suspects sensed the same disturbing quiet whenever they entered a room. And why didn't Julian sit with her at the prospectives' dinner last night? She'd been so disappointed when she spotted him clear across the room, with some of the squash guys. But maybe he just hadn't seen her sitting there, and then hadn't been able to move once Marymount began his speech.

"Okay, you're still not relaxed. Let's try something else. Close your eyes." Mrs. Silver put one freshly lotioned hand over Jenny's eyes for effect. "Good. Now pick up the pencil and just start drawing. Don't think about it. Just move the pencil over the canvas."

Jenny was sure everyone was staring at her, but she went along with the exercise. The scent of Mrs. Silver's rose-hip lotion filled her nose. Her arm moved rapidly, like a lie detector needle in a movie when the suspect is telling wild lies. Soon her wrist was getting in on the action, adding a detail here and there while Jenny studied the inside of her eyelids. Mrs. Silver removed her hand and Jenny kept her eyes closed. The light passing through her eyelids made her see nothing but red.

"Good," Mrs. Silver urged. "You've got it now. Think of it as taking your brain out of the equation—just let your subconscious speak directly through your pencil. Keep doing it—keep your eyes closed if you need to."

Jenny heard Mrs. Silver walk away to talk to another student at the front of the room. She opened her eyes again, but instead of looking at what was on the paper, she stared out the enormous plate glass windows of the art studio, watching the heavy wind whip through the bright red leaves of the birch trees directly outside. Rain droplets started to fall, splattering against the windows along with a few stray leaves.

After what seemed like a very long time had passed, Jenny pulled herself from her trance, hearing Alison, a couple of desks away, snap her supply bin closed with a bang. Jenny's eyes rested on her own drawing. She paused. Had she actually drawn this? The sketch pad in front of her was filled with messy dark lines, but the scene itself was clear. A thinly sketched building, the entire top of which was consumed in dancing, leaping flames, while on the ground dark figures ran in all directions. Jenny focused on two figures that seemed to remain stationary, oblivious to the fire, locked in a squiggly embrace amid the chaos. The figures were recognizable only to Jenny.

In an instant, the entire ordeal replayed itself in Jenny's head. Easy and Callie had hooked up behind her back. Callie had betrayed her promise of friendship. And Easy had told her before they even got together that things with Callie had been over for a long time. Another lie.

"Wow, that's intense." Alison leaned in and inspected Jenny's drawing, her smooth black hair falling forward and tickling Jenny's bare forearm.

Jenny snapped back to reality. "Thanks."

"I'm not even sure what mine's supposed to be." Alison shrugged at her sketch pad, which was filled with a series of dots and squiggly lines floating around a rectangle. "My subconscious is way less interesting than yours."

Jenny stared at her drawing, swearing she could hear the crackle of the barn burning down and smell the charred wood. She was thankful she'd "tapped into her subconscious" in portraiture class, the only art class she didn't share with Easy.

"So who do you think is going to get the ax?" Alison asked under her breath.

Jenny trained her eyes on the figures at the center of her drawing, remembering Callie's bare skin, Easy's hands traveling the length of Callie's skinny body. "Callie and Easy were the only ones actually in the barn. And they were smoking." Jenny shrugged. "That's what I heard, anyway."

"Do you think they'll *both* get kicked out?" Alison whispered.

Jenny was suddenly aware of someone behind her, and had the eerie feeling that she was being watched. She deliberately dropped her pencil and reached down to retrieve it, glancing over her shoulder. But it was only Chloe, looking innocuous in a yellow-striped Ralph Lauren polo dress and doodling with a piece of charcoal. She'd been so silent throughout class that Jenny had forgotten she was there. Mrs. Silver was right—she really needed to relax. She was getting paranoid. "Maybe," Jenny replied.

"I just want Marymount's interrogation meeting to be over with." Alison sighed. "It's so stressful. It's making me totally break out." She pointed toward her cheek, where an almost invisible pimple lingered below her left eye. It looked like a freckle.

"Where are we going next?" Chloe suddenly piped up, and Jenny nearly fell out of her seat. She needed to drink some chamomile tea. Or find Julian. He knew how to relax her.

"Um, I'm supposed to go meet Alan. . . ." Alison glanced at Jenny guiltily and the girls packed up their pencils and headed to the supply shelves.

"How about I go with Jenny, then?" Chloe asked eagerly, her blond ponytail bobbing as she followed them.

Jenny began to shake her head no—she didn't have the energy to squire around a prospective—but then she felt guilty. "Yeah, you can hang out with me." After all, she knew a little too well what it felt like to be lost at Waverly.

JennyHumphrey: I've got a prospective attached to my hip. Want to help me entertain her?

JulianMcCafferty: Sure thing.

JennyHumphrey: Meet us at the coffee bar in Maxwell after class?

JulianMcCafferty: How 'bout we go off campus instead? Ritoli's?

JennyHumphrey: Mmm, pizza. It's a date.

BrandonBuchanan: Hey, fellow Usual Suspect. How's it going?

SageFrancis: It's okay. . . . Feeling a little freaked out though . . .

BrandonBuchanan: Why I got in touch. Hoping to commiserate.

SageFrancis: Think we should plan our alibis for tomorrow?

BrandonBuchanan: It's the most we can do, right?

SageFrancis: Right. I'll scratch your back if you scratch mine.

BrandonBuchanan: I'd be up for that. Could offer your back a little massage, too. See you at the party tonight?

SageFrancis: I'll be there.

**DOORS MUST REMAIN OPEN AT ALL TIMES DURING
APPROVED OPPOSITE-SEX DORM VISITATION HOURS.**

Brett rapped her knuckles against Kara's closed door, her turquoise-and-scarlet beaded bracelets clinking together. Yvonne Stidder had left a note on Kara's dry-erase message board asking if she wanted to have lunch. It was funny—in all the recent insanity, Brett had almost forgotten that anyone other than Kara and the other Usual Suspects even existed.

The past few days had reminded Brett of the floor-to-ceiling aquariums in the foyer of her parents' McMansion. You could always tell when one of the tetras or rainbow fish was sick, because all the other fish would avoid them, as though the scent of death were clinging to them. Brett felt like one of the sick fish. But she wasn't the only one. Behind closed doors or surrounded by whispers, she was positive the other "suspects" were drawing up alliances, calling on old friendships and favors in order to protect themselves from whatever wrath Dean Marymount was ready to unleash. Which was why she needed Kara now. She'd felt pretty panicked since her chat with Mr. Tomkins yesterday and wanted to get their stories straight.

"Come in."

She pushed open Kara's door. Heath Ferro was sprawled next to Kara on her bed, his head resting in her cross-legged lap while she braided his dirty blond hair. Um, what?

Heath's prospective protégé reclined on the blue vinyl beanbag in the corner, his tiny legs propped up against the window, holding an open Batgirl comic book over his face. Probably trying to imagine what Batgirl looked like without her costume on. A Beastie Boys song played on Kara's sound dock, and everyone seemed quietly absorbed in what they were doing. Given the serene, domestic-bliss feel of the scene, Brett wouldn't have been surprised if classical music came on next.

"Another prayer answered." Heath's eyes lit up. He sat up quickly and scooted over, little half braids sticking out all over his head as he made room on the Batgirl comforter between him and Kara.

Brett sat gingerly on the bed. "So . . ." She looked first at Kara and then at Heath. "What are you guys up to?" Since when did Kara and Heath have hair-braiding sessions?

"I'm acting as a consultant for the party tonight." Kara smiled, tucking her legs underneath her. She wore a flouncy polka-dot skirt that splayed out on the comforter like a tutu. "Heath had some *very* important questions he needed answered,"

she added, turning to Heath, who winked back at her. In the
Waverly T-shirt he'd been wearing since Marymount sent out
the suspect list (a tongue-in-cheek effort to show his school
spirit) and his worn-out Citizens of Humanity jeans, Heath
looked like the quintessential smug prep-school boy.

"Don't you guys think we should be, like, planning our
alibis instead of planning a kegger?" Brett stood up. She pulled
down on the bottom of her white Reyes button-up and turned
to face Kara and Heath on the bed.

"A party always trumps a trial in my mind," Heath said
with a lazy grin, scratching his stomach through his T-shirt.
"Come on, Marymount's 'list' is such bull." He made air quotes
around the word *list*. "I'm seeing it for what it really is: an
excuse to get drunk and miss class." He reached a hand out for
Sam to slap. "Right on, son!"

Brett just stared at him. Heath and his don't-give-a-shit
attitude. Didn't he realize how serious this whole thing was?
One of them could be gone *tomorrow*.

"So you don't even want to talk about what *we* were doing
at the party?" Brett asked challengingly. She put her hands on
the hips of her 7 For All Mankind jeans and locked eyes with
Heath, not daring to look at Kara.

"Sam, buddy." Heath turned his half-braided head toward
his Mini Me. "Grab some hallway, will you? I need some alone
time with my girls."

Sam popped up from the beanbag, looking like he was about
to salute Heath. "The pony express rides again!" he hailed in
his surprisingly deep voice. He held out his hand for a high five

from Heath, but Heath kicked out his leg instead, directing Sam toward the door.

"What do you think is going to happen in here?" Brett blocked Sam's exit, still staring at Heath. "That we're going to have some sort of orgy?" She had meant it as a joke, but there was a hard edge to her voice that she couldn't control.

"Relax, baby," Heath said, still smiling, his green eyes shining. "You've got to loosen up."

Kara giggled nervously, like she wasn't sure what to do. She took off her glasses and looked up at Brett, her head tilted slightly, as if trying to figure out what was going on.

"I *did* loosen up." Brett couldn't stop herself. "And look what's happened." She'd meant the comment for Heath, but Kara blinked several times and looked as if she'd just been slapped. Brett wanted to apologize. But with Heath and his little Mini Me hanging on her every word, all she could do was back out of the room, not bothering to close the door behind her.

Kara followed her out into the hallway, gently closing the door to her room behind them. "What's going on?" Her hazel eyes were filled with concern. Now that her eyes were no longer obscured by glasses, Brett noticed her delicate dark lashes, which were long and curly, even though she wore no mascara.

Brett shrugged her shoulders and fiddled with the pearly buttons on her shirt. She wanted to tell Kara about what had happened in Dean Marymount's office yesterday, about how worried she was. She knew that they'd done nothing wrong— they'd had nothing to do with the fire, and kissing another girl was hardly against the rules—but she also knew that once they got into that interrogation room, anything could happen. They really *could* get kicked out of Waverly, if someone wanted them gone. But she didn't trust herself to say anything else right then. "I'm gonna go take a nap. I'll see you at the party later."

"Are you sure you don't want to come back in?" Kara tilted her head back toward the doorway. An Amy Winehouse song Brett liked was now filtering through the door. "I snagged some peanut butter cookies from the dining hall for you." She smiled hopefully.

Brett shook her head. "Nah, seems like you guys were having more fun without me anyway." She turned on her heel and made her way down the dark hallway, not looking back to see the hurt expression on Kara's face.

16

A WAVERLY OWL TICKLES A FELLOW OWL ONLY
AFTER A PROPER INVITATION.

Brandon let the depressing sounds of Wilco wash over him as he lay on his bed, thinking about the dean's suspect list. He was going to need a better alibi than "I was too busy telling off my girlfriend of five minutes to start the fire." Marymount would probably make him reenact the scene with Elizabeth in front of everyone, and for the rest of Brandon's tenure at Waverly people would whisper, "Mr. Open is closed," and snicker whenever he walked past. Fuck. At least Sage Francis had seemed receptive to his IMs earlier. It was sort of cowardly to approach a girl via text message, but you couldn't blame a guy for testing the waters. After all, what if that prospective girl Chloe had heard wrong? He didn't need another disaster of Elizabethan proportions. This time, his motto was "Slow and cautious." He'd planted the seed, and tonight at Heath's alcohol-drenched party, he'd attempt to water it.

A drumbeat came out of nowhere, trampling the lead vocals of his favorite song. It took him a minute to realize it wasn't a drum at all, but someone knocking on his door. If it was fucking Sam again, he was going to kill him—but then Sam apparently wasn't the knocking type. He'd stormed through the door at seven-thirty that morning while Brandon was still toweling off from his shower, asking Brandon snidely what color dress he'd be wearing today. Goddamn little Heath clone.

The door swung open. Sage Francis was standing in his doorway, wearing a short wool houndstooth Chanel dress, her long pale blond hair clipped out of her face with two tiny dragonfly-shaped yellow sequined barrettes.

"Hey," he said, trying not to betray his surprise. He ran his fingers through his hair, suddenly self-conscious about his plain white Hanes undershirt—was it pit-stained?—and grateful for his still-crisp pair of charcoal gray Theory trousers.

"Hi." Sage smiled confidently. Brandon had always thought of Sage as one of Callie's generic, giggling friends. But on her own, framed in his doorway, she looked . . . different.

"So, uh . . . how's it going?" Brandon asked casually. His slow and cautious method was one thing, but he hadn't been prepared for an ambush. He glanced around the room sheepishly, hoping she wouldn't notice the pair of Heath's polka-dotted boxer shorts on the floor near his bed where he'd left them. Or, if she did, he hoped she at least wouldn't think they were his.

Sage shrugged her shoulders. "After our chat earlier, I

thought I'd drop in." She nodded at the Latin textbook lying facedown on Brandon's neatly made bed, on top of his Ralph Lauren down comforter. He quickly smoothed out the wrinkles where he'd been lying and sat up. "Studying?"

Brandon shook his head no, although he did have a Latin recitation in the morning. Apparently he was going to miss it for Marymount's US meeting. Not exactly a fair trade. "*Thinking* about studying." Sage giggled, and Brandon felt emboldened. "Come on in." He was grateful when she left the door open—at least some of Heath's disgusting sweaty gorilla-man odor would vent into the hall.

"I have a geometry test on Thursday, but it's a little hard to study for it, knowing I might be expelled before then." Sage sat down on the edge of Brandon's unmade bed. There was something about the way she perched on the corner of the bed, his white chenille throw blanket swirling around her tanned legs, that made Brandon suddenly sit up a little straighter.

"Come on. Why would you be expelled?" Brandon demanded. "You didn't have anything to do with the fire." He hoped that didn't come out as a question. Because he really doubted she did. With her wispy, corn silk blond hair and bright blue eyes, it seemed next to impossible Sage could do something so devious. She was the picture of innocence. He envisioned her with wings on a Hallmark card.

Sage shrugged her shoulders again and ran her fingers over a snag in the blanket that Brandon had never noticed. "Well, I'm on the list."

"*Everyone's* on the list." Brandon waved his hand casually, hoping that it was a leading-man, reassuring gesture. If he had made up the list, it would have had only a few people on it: Tinsley—because really, who else would be wicked enough to start a fire—and Easy Walsh, just because Brandon wouldn't mind seeing him get expelled. Even if he had started to think Easy wasn't such a bad guy after all, he couldn't help recalling the image of Easy and Callie running, barely clothed, from the barn. He doubted they'd do anything intentionally, but they were the only people who were in the barn for sure. And he really didn't love the idea that his ex-girlfriend was doing the deed with Easy Walsh, in a *barn* of all places. Gross. He was totally over Callie, but a girl like that deserved one-thousand-thread-count Egyptian cotton sheets for her first time—if the rumors about what they were doing in there were actually true, and not just a bale of hay.

"You're not worried?" Sage asked incredulously, her small mouth dropping open so that Brandon could see one neat silver filling in a molar. She rocked back and forth, smoothing a strand of her fine blond hair off her forehead. Brandon briefly wondered whether she'd want to hook up in a barn—she seemed more the white lace, canopy bed type. Much more Brandon's style.

"Great dress," Brandon blurted, realizing he'd been staring at Sage's slender legs. *Great dress!* It sounded pretty innocuous, and who wouldn't want to hear that they were wearing a great dress? But he sounded totally gay.

"Bought it at a thrift store," she admitted, running a finger lightly over the hem.

"Wow." Brandon lowered his voice and raised his eyebrows

in surprise. "Scandal," he noted. Girls had this weird thing about vintage being so much cooler than new. He didn't get it. Vintage clothes just meant that someone had already sweated in them.

"You couldn't even imagine." Sage looked up at him through her long eyelashes, feigning embarrassment. "It's actually from this totally random church yard sale in Great Barrington."

Brandon laughed. He remembered vaguely that Sage's family were some sort of ceramics barons in western Massachusetts, but now he had the endearing image of her pawing through racks of old-lady clothes in some old stone church basement, searching for Chanel dresses. It was very un-Waverly, and totally cute.

"Don't tell anyone, okay?" Her voice was sugared with irony and she leaned forward conspiratorially. Brandon had to restrain himself for sneaking a peek down the front of her dress.

"Got any other secrets?" He ran his fingers through his gold-brown hair, raising an eyebrow suggestively.

"My second toe is longer than my big toe," Sage answered immediately, kicking up her feet playfully and sucking her cheeks in.

"They say that's the mark of genius. Lemme see." Brandon reached forward, pretending to grab for Sage's black suede Moschino Cheap & Chic wedges, but she giggled and quickly folded her legs beneath her. The bed bounced violently, the up and down motion and accompanying squeaking noise scandalizing them both for a moment, before they started to laugh.

"You can't just grab a girl's feet," she told him coquettishly, her face a little flushed. "You have to earn it."

Brandon turned to face her, smiling. "And how do—" He was cut off by Heath's sudden appearance in the doorway, with his wannabe prospective close on his heels.

"Oh, sorry." Heath's chest was heaving and his gray, faded Waverly T-shirt clung to his chest like cling wrap. It looked like someone had started braiding his hair but then quit mid-effort, and little braids stuck up all over his head like weeds in a garden. "Dude, Sam's gonna chill out with you for a bit."

"But I wanna go with *you*," Sam protested. Sam had on a Waverly T-shirt as well, but it was starchy and looked like it had been purchased just this morning from one of the little stores that sold all things Waverly in downtown Rhinecliff. Brandon glanced at Sage, who giggled at the sight of Heath and Sam and scooted off the bed, tugging down the hem of her fitted dress.

"Dude, you almost got me killed back there. Just stay here." Heath turned to Brandon. "I gotta get some things ready for the party tonight and can't have him in the way. Make sure he stays here." Heath disappeared down the hall and Sam ran off after him. It seemed that Heath had displaced even the PSP at the top of Sam's list of priorities.

Sage stepped toward the door, slowly, her wispy blond hair falling down over her shoulders. "I should . . . uh . . . probably go anyway?"

"Oh, okay." He nodded, not sure if he should try to stop her. He was grateful Heath and Sam had disappeared for at least a few seconds so he could say goodbye without them nosing around. "But I'll see you at the party later, right?"

She glanced over her shoulder and flashed him a flirty smile. "Right."

The door closed and Brandon lay back down on his plaid comforter, running his bare feet over the soft throw blanket Sage had been sitting on. It was still warm. If he was lucky, Sage would get into the now-or-never spirit of the party tonight. And so would he.

SageFrancis: Brandon is making my job way too easy.

AlisonQuentin: Seriously? I told you so.

SageFrancis: A girl can hope. . . .

AlisonQuentin: Let's just hope we're all still here tomorrow to enjoy our boys.

SageFrancis: Wow, you just stomped all over my good mood. ☹

AlisonQuentin: Only kidding! Don't worry, Brandon will cheer you up tonight.

17

A WISE OWL KNOWS FLIRTING IS EVEN MORE FUN WHEN OTHER OWLS ARE WATCHING.

"Pineapple, peanut butter, and pistachios," Julian answered, making a face for Chloe's benefit, but Jenny couldn't help giggling along. "Okay, my turn. Lemme think of a hard one." He scrunched his face up in concentration. "How about *M?* And you can't say 'meat.'"

"Time me," Chloe said, up to the challenge of naming three gross pizza toppings that started with the letter *M.* Julian looked at his bare wrist and said, "Go."

"Marshmallows . . ." Chloe's voice trailed off as she struggled to come up with another answer. Jenny watched Julian's delight in stumping Chloe. She was glad Julian had suggested getting pizza at Ritoli's, far from the madding crowd of whispering Owls. It was nice to get the smell of freshly polished hardwood floors out of their noses and replace it with the yummy smell of pizza.

Ritoli's was a family-run business that had been in down-town Rhinecliff for years. It probably got half of its business from the late-night delivery orders from Waverly boys—and the other half from the in-person visits of Waverly girls. It was a favorite with female Owls because there were always cute Italian pizza boys working, all olive-skinned and toned and ready to take orders. Not that Jenny was interested in that today—she was much more interested in the tall, shaggy-haired boy sitting across from her.

"Macadamia nuts!" Chloe shouted out suddenly, alarming the couple at the booth next to them. "Yes, that's a good one!" she said excitedly.

"I wouldn't take time to stop and brag," Julian warned, pointing at his phantom watch. "It's almost been half an hour."

"No, it hasn't!" Chloe appealed to Jenny, anxiously clinking the bottom of her fork against the red-and-white-checked tablecloth.

Jenny shrugged her shoulders, clamping her hand over her red plastic watch. She was wearing her favorite black Jill Stuart puff-sleeved T-shirt and her paint-splattered pencil-leg Antik Denim jeans, and she felt pretty, confident, and relaxed. Or maybe it was Julian who made her feel that way.

"You guys are cheating," Chloe admonished, though she was quickly distracted by the appearance of their waiter, who set a steaming pan of gooey cheese-and-mushroom pizza down in front of them. Luckily, it was a waiter Jenny had never seen before. She was relieved that Angelo, the pizza boy Tinsley had

forced to play spin-the-bottle at the last Café Society meeting—
a phony cool-girl exclusive society Tinsley had attempted to
form that died before it even got off the ground—was nowhere
to be seen.

Julian arched one eyebrow at Jenny, like a villain in the
Masterpiece Theatre Saturday afternoon movies her father sometimes watched on PBS. The whole outing made Jenny feel like
she was in one of those romantic comedies where the single mom
tests her potential suitor by bringing her annoying child out on a
date. Julian was clearly enjoying his role of entertaining Chloe—
maybe too much. Chloe was totally flirting with him.

Not that Jenny blamed her. Wearing a thin yellow plaid
Abercrombie & Fitch button-down over a red T-shirt with a
picture of Snoopy lying on a globe, the words SAVE OUR PLANET
curved under it, Julian looked totally irresistible.

"Go, go, go!" Julian spurred Chloe on, while trying to fluster
her, too. Jenny remembered how her older brother, Dan, would
use the same strategy to psych her out during family games of
Boggle and Scrabble—and it always worked. Julian had mentioned two younger sisters, so of course he was an expert at
torturing them. "Five seconds and I win. Five, four . . ."

"Okay, I got one. Stop counting."

"Three and a half, three . . ." Julian dug a piece of deep-dish
mushroom pizza out of the pan and scooped it onto a plate. He
handed it to Jenny with a grin.

"I'm not going to tell you until you stop counting." Chloe
crossed her tiny arms, pouting. She gave Julian a half smile of
thanks when he dished her out a piece, too.

"Two and a half . . ."

Jenny took a bite of steaming pizza, hoping the gooey cheese wouldn't stick to her face. Having served both girls, Julian shoveled two slices onto his plate.

"Two and a quarter . . ." Julian tapped his finger to his bare wrist to signal that time was up.

"Maraschino cherries!" Chloe blurted out, looking pleased with herself. Jenny was surprised by how much attitude the girl seemed to muster when she wasn't around Benny and Sage and those girls. She could probably do pretty well for herself at Waverly. Wearing a black Banana Republic cashmere cardigan, she was even starting to look more like a Waverly girl and less like she'd exploded from an L.L.Bean catalog.

Julian made a buzzing sound. "Sorry, but thanks for playing," he said in a TV show announcer's voice. "It's Marciano cherries, not maraschino."

"What? That's not true. I need a judge's ruling on that," Chloe countered, appealing again to Jenny. Her normally pale face was flushed.

Jenny was a little afraid they'd wound Chloe up beyond control, so she took the middle road. "I honestly don't know." She shrugged.

Chloe threw her hands up, exasperated. She looked around wildly and Jenny worried for a moment that she was going to ask the couple they'd disrupted earlier. But instead Chloe flagged down the nearest waiter, who happened to be Angelo, much to Jenny's embarrassment.

"What do you call those little cherries that taste like candy?"

Chloe inquired. Angelo focused on Jenny, as if he were trying to remember her name, or place her face, and Jenny slouched in the booth a little, giving him a polite smile before turning her face away to look at the menu board over the kitchen.

"I don't know," Angelo said, twirling his empty serving tray on his index finger, "but we don't have them."

The argument spilled out onto the street after the bill was paid. "*Marciano* is Rocky's last name, dummy," Chloe mocked Julian, who was walking backward in front of her.

He began dancing around Chloe with his fists in the air. "Adrienne!" he called out, mimicking Stallone's famous cry, the people on the streets of Rhinecliff stopping to stare. Jenny giggled, and Julian quickly turned on her, touching his fist lightly against her arm. He held it there for a second longer than necessary.

"Not the Rocky in the movie, the real-life one," Chloe chastised, rolling her eyes as if Julian were truly ridiculous. "Oh cool," she said, distracted by the stained glass lamp that rotated in the window of the Knick-Knack Shack, Rhinecliff's local junk store. Waverly kids liked to shop at the Knick-Knack Shack for ironic dorm furniture, like coasters made from old '45s. It shared an entrance with Next-to-New, the thrift store that everyone at Waverly called Not So New. Jenny spotted a pair of cool '80s white leather slouch ankle boots. "I'm gonna go check it out—I'll be right back," Chloe announced, marching into the store before they could stop her.

Jenny turned to Julian, glad to have a momentary break from Chloe. "Pizza was a good idea. Thanks for dragging me off campus." She shielded her eyes from the harsh afternoon sun, wondering what she'd done with her scratched-up aviator sunglasses. "I think I was going a little stir-crazy."

"My pleasure." Julian took a gallant bow, his open Abercrombie shirt fluttering out to the sides. Even doubled over, he was taller than she was. "Only the best for my best girl."

Jenny giggled. "I thought maybe you wanted to go off campus because you were hiding me from your other girlfriend."

Julian straightened, his shaggy brown-blond hair flopping around his head. The blood had rushed to his head and his face was a bit flushed. "Yeah, she gets pretty jealous. I have to keep a low profile," he teased, leaning against the store window.

"Which was why you hid in broom closets and behind bushes around my dorm to talk to me?" Jenny cocked her head flirtatiously, her dark curls bouncing. She wasn't sure what it was about Julian, but he made her feel giddy and reckless and yet still safe.

"You see right through me." He nodded, a smile curling his handsome lips. He leaned forward and then took a peek into the Knick-Knack Shop. Jenny hoped he was making sure Chloe wasn't around so he could kiss her.

She looked up at Julian, unable to wipe the grin from her face. She couldn't believe it—Julian had liked her all along, and had even *arranged* to meet her. Nothing could feel better than this. He was so cute, so funny, so sweet . . . which, Jenny realized, were all qualities that had drawn her to Easy.

But unlike Easy, she knew Julian would never lie to her.

From: TinsleyCarmichael@waverly.edu
To: chloe.marymount@gmail.com
Date: Tuesday, October 15, 6:09 P.M.
Subject: How's it going?

Hey Chloe,

Hope you had a good day. Just thought I'd see if you wanted to get ready together for the party tonight. . . .

Tinsley

From: chloe.marymount@gmail.com
To: TinsleyCarmichael@waverly.edu
Date: Tuesday, October 15, 6:11 P.M.
Subject: RE: How's it going?

Ohmigod Tinsley, I'd totally love to. Can't wait!

XOXOXOX

Chloe

P.S. What are you wearing? Think I could borrow something?

A WAVERLY OWL DOES NOT BAD-MOUTH HIS GIRLFRIEND TO HER EX.

"Do you really just read books all day long? You never play video games?" Sam threw Heath's PSP on the bed and looked at Brandon expectantly.

"Yes," Brandon said tersely, hoping Sam would leave him alone. He was ready to put down his copy of *Great Expectations*—which he was more than ready to put down anyway—and take a squash racket to Sam's already-battered nose.

"If you don't have any more games, can we at least go see some girls?"

Brandon was still seething at Heath for dumping Sam on him. And still reeling from the fact that Sage Francis had appeared in his doorway, a vision of loveliness in her Jackie O dress and smooth, pin-straight blond hair, and proceeded to flirt with him. Sage Francis. And all he'd had to do was send her a few text messages. Who knew girls could be so simple?

Definitely not Heath, who'd filled his protégé's head with all kinds of crazy ideas.

"Okay, let's go somewhere." Brandon stood up and pulled his black Hugo Boss hooded sweater on over his plain white American Apparel T-shirt. He grabbed his worn leather Prada wallet and slid it into the pocket of his charcoal trousers.

"To see some girls?" Sam hopped up and stood in front of Heath's mirror, adjusting the gelled spikes in his light brown hair. "I like that one that was in here before. Sage? She's got great legs."

Brandon walked out the door, shaking his head. Where was he going to take this tool? As he marched down the hallway, he passed Easy Walsh's half-open door. Of course—Easy and Alan St. Girard were up most nights playing Xbox for hours after lights-out, the volume on mute while occasional groans or cheers emitted from their room as they killed aliens or kick-boxed street thugs or whatever brainless task was required in those games. Brandon knocked on the door, taking a deep breath and trying not to think about the rumors that Callie and Easy had actually slept together.

There was a pause, and then a sleepy voice called out, "Yeah?"

"You got Wii?" Sam asked, pushing Brandon aside and poking his head in the door to scout the dorm room for its gaming system.

Easy was on his back on his bed, in a pair of torn jeans and a ratty-looking green sweater, his American history textbook facedown on his chest. "What?" he asked, propping himself up on his elbows. Then he shook his head. "Nah, I've got an Xbox . . . but it's broken right now." Sam's face lit up and fell immediately.

"He's looking for some new games," Brandon said apologetically.

"I have to go into town to get some charcoal pencils," Easy said, rubbing his sleepy-looking blue eyes with his hand. "You guys can tag along if you want." Sam seemed unimpressed, until Easy added, "There's an arcade."

"Cool," Sam squealed like the true thirteen-year-old boy he was, his mini-Heath persona momentarily forgotten.

They strolled to Rhinecliff side by side, Easy on one side of Sam and Brandon on the other, a wide gap between each. Brandon remained silent as Easy and Sam discussed the merits and drawbacks of Xbox versus PlayStation versus Wii. The smell of rain hung in the air and Brandon wished he hadn't worn his good John Varvatos suede loafers.

"Which one of you is better at House of the Dead 4?" Sam piped up as the main street of downtown Rhinecliff came into view. It was a warm Tuesday afternoon, and the sidewalks were swarming with students and their corresponding prospectives. The hippie guy some of the kids—Heath included—occasionally bought weed from was manning a table of neatly folded tie-dye shirts in every color imaginable. Brandon highly doubted the students crowded around his table were there to buy T-shirts.

He gave Easy a sideways glance and Easy returned it, cracking a smile. "I've never even *heard* of that game," Brandon said, scanning the crowd for familiar faces. He thought he spotted Jenny up ahead, looking in the window of the thrift shop. Her hair was loose and fell down her back in lush, dark curls. How could Easy have broken up with her?

"C'mon." Sam kicked at a loose stone, sending it skittering toward one of the hunter green BMWs parked on the street. They rounded a corner and stood facing the arcade, its flashing lights visible through the windows. Sam's eyes lit up greedily. "Who wants to play me first?"

"Who's buying?" Easy asked mischievously, his thumbs hooked into the pockets of his paint-splattered jeans. Did he own any articles of clothing that weren't splattered with paint? Two weeks ago, Brandon would have suspected Easy of intentionally spilling paint on himself in strategic spots—a splotch of red on the knee, three drips of green on the left thigh, a smudge of black on his sleeve—in order to appear as endearingly arty to girls as possible. But over the past week or so, with Easy acting like a decent human being to him, Brandon was ready to give him the benefit of the doubt. He was clearly just a slob.

"You guys got quarters, right?" Sam asked.

Brandon shook out his empty pockets. "Nada."

Sam's face fell as Easy shrugged his shoulders. "Guess I'll have to break a twenty." Sam sighed.

"I bet you can buy tokens at the arcade," Easy reasoned. He pulled his phone from his pocket and glanced at it, probably to see if he had any messages from Callie.

"Are you kidding me?" Sam responded, sounding horrified. He checked his hair in the giant plate glass window of the Rhinecliff Community Bank, just next door to the arcade. "The rates are terrible. Tokens are for suckers. You *have* to bring your own quarters." He stuck his thumb in the direction of the bank. "I'm going in."

Brandon and Easy waited outside while Sam stood in the long line at the bank for quarters. They shuffled their feet awkwardly on the sidewalk.

"I'm going to run over to the pharmacy and get my pencils," Easy announced suddenly, clearly as desperate to avoid awkward silences as Brandon was. He stepped off the sidewalk and into the street.

Brandon nodded slowly. The pharmacy was the only place in town to get all kinds of necessities, and they did have a huge aisle of school supplies—but still, he couldn't help wondering if Easy was really going to stock up on condoms.

"Hey," Easy said suddenly, patting his hand against the pack of Marlboro Reds half sticking out of his pocket. "Sorry things didn't work out with Elizabeth. I heard about what happened. Think you did the right thing, though."

Brandon searched Easy's face for a smirk, but Easy looked totally sincere. "Thanks," he said. "It does kind of suck."

"Maybe she'll come around." Easy shrugged. The sun came out from behind a cloud, lighting up the gray afternoon sky. He pulled a pair of brandless black aviators from the collar of his green wool sweater. The sleeves were too short. "You never know."

"Yeah," Brandon said, looking down the street for Jenny

again, but she was gone. "It was just . . . too impossible." *Impossible* was the right word, wasn't it? Maybe not. It was theoretically possible for Brandon to become one of Elizabeth's rotating cast of boyfriends, crossing his fingers that he'd be the one to get the call for Friday or Saturday night, sometimes settling for a Wednesday lunch or a Monday movie, but it wasn't *realistic*. Maybe that was a good answer when people asked: "It wasn't realistic." And it definitely wasn't what he wanted.

A beat passed and then Brandon added, "Heard you and Callie worked it out, though." Easy nodded, though Brandon noticed with interest that Easy seemed to nod tentatively, as if he wasn't sure. As if to avoid looking Brandon in the eye, Easy pulled the pack of cigarettes from his pocket. He flicked open a book of matches, stuck a cigarette between his lips, and lit it in one smooth motion. "That's cool," Brandon said.

"Yeah." Easy inhaled a deep breath of smoke, wondering if smoking in public was really the smartest thing for him to be doing right now. Well, fuck it. Marymount was probably too excited about tomorrow morning's meeting to be doing any shopping downtown. Besides, it felt good to be outside. As soon as he'd left the Staxxx this morning, his uneasy feelings had returned, and he'd spent all afternoon cooped up in his room worrying. The more he thought about it, the more it seemed like Callie *was* plotting something—and he wouldn't be surprised if Tinsley was behind it all. "Have you, uh, talked to her?"

An elderly woman passed between them and Brandon opened the bank door for her. She smiled kindly at Brandon, then took one glance at Easy's cigarette and shot him a scowl over her shoulder. "To Callie? No, not recently."

"Oh." Easy didn't know how to bring the whole thing up without sounding like he was ratting Callie out to Brandon. He took another drag of his cigarette, old ladies be damned.

"Why?" Brandon asked curiously. This conversation was getting sort of creepily random. Why was Easy asking *him* about Callie?

Easy shifted his feet and sighed. "I just wondered if you knew what she was up to."

"Is she up to something?"

"Well, everyone seems to be pointing fingers at me and her about the fire"—he rushed the phrase together so as not to get into a subject neither of them wanted to discuss—"and I'm worried she's going to do something drastic to try to, like, save the day."

Brandon laughed, smoothing out a wrinkle in his dark gray trousers. "Like what? Do something even worse to create a distraction?" He leaned against the brick wall of the bank. "Seduce the dean? That's not exactly her style."

Easy smiled despite himself, kicking a foot against the curb. "No, it's not. I just have this weird feeling that she's up to something, and that Tinsley's involved."

"Those two don't need any help getting into trouble," Brandon remarked. A couple of sophomore girls headed toward the ATM machine giggled shyly as they passed by.

Easy glanced through the giant, freshly Windexed bank window, trying to gauge Sam's progress in the line and how much time they had left. "I'm worried it's a scheme against Jenny," he blurted out. He'd come to that conclusion this afternoon. If Callie was convinced Jenny had started the fire and was going to be sent home, it wasn't too much of a stretch to think that she'd help speed the process along. And if there was a scheme in the works at Waverly, you could bet that Tinsley Carmichael was the mastermind. It would explain everything: Callie's hushed conversation with Tinsley in the stables the other day, Callie and Tinsley's reestablished friendship, Callie's confidence that they wouldn't be the ones to go home.

Brandon put his hands in his pockets and looked him straight in the eye. He raised a golden-brown eyebrow. "Jenny?"

"Yeah, I know it's crazy, but I keep coming back to that same idea. I . . ." Easy's voice trailed off. His dry throat felt like it would crack if he kept talking, but he wanted to confess to someone. "I feel like I screwed Jenny over. And I don't want this on top of it." As happy as Easy was to be back together with Callie, the girl he loved, he still felt terrible about how he'd dumped Jenny to get back with Callie.

"If you think you screwed her over," Brandon said slowly, in a tone that sounded like he was trying very hard not to be judgmental, "then why don't you just say you're sorry?" At five feet eight inches and standing on the sidewalk, with Easy still on the street, Brandon was about the same height as Easy, and their eyes were exactly level.

"Maybe I will," Easy conceded, mulling it over. It sounded so simple. But apologies were never simple. Two years of dating Callie had taught him that. "Thanks. I owe you one," he added.

"Get my back tomorrow," Brandon joked.

Easy nodded gravely, stepping up onto the sidewalk beside Brandon. "Deal."

They shook hands again and Easy headed off toward the pharmacy, a little bounce in his step. Maybe things would turn out all right in the end. Maybe he was just being paranoid. Callie and Tinsley couldn't seriously be trying to pin the fire on Jenny. Callie would never go that far. Would she?

Because that would mean the girl he loved with all his heart was, well, not the kind of person he *wanted* to be in love with.

JennyHumphrey: You going to the Goodbye US party?

BrettMessershmidt: Yup. Just getting out of the shower. You?

JennyHumphrey: On my way over. Get here quick! I can't face this alone.

BrettMesserschmidt: Ditto. But don't worry—that's what booze is for.

A WAVERLY OWL GRACIOUSLY FORGIVES, EVEN
IF SHE CAN'T FORGET.

As Jenny approached the Crater, the venue of choice for the Goodbye US party, she couldn't help but compare parties at Waverly to those in Manhattan. Back home, they sipped cocktails at bars in the Meatpacking District or attended galas at the Met. Well, at least some people did—Jenny was only occasionally invited. At Waverly, the parties were more of the outdoor-adventure variety. The Crater was a grassy depression a couple of hundred feet into the woods, just south of campus. The site was close enough to skip class and grab a smoke, but far enough away to not get busted. Over the years, enterprising Waverly students had arranged logs into benches that lined the Crater, so that the whole thing looked like some kind of medieval holy meeting ground. Attending a party there was a bit like going to a party at Stonehenge.

Tonight, Heath had really outdone himself. There were

heated tents along the rim of the Crater, so that it looked like a classy version of the Depression-era shantytowns Jenny had learned about in American history. The whole place was over-run with students in red, orange, and yellow clothing, as if everyone had had the same idea. A small bonfire crackled at the center of the Crater, casting flickering shadows on everyone's faces so that it was hard to make out who was who. It was sort of a romantic setting actually, and Jenny couldn't wait until Julian showed up so they could be a cheesy couple and stare into each other's eyes as they kissed by the fire.

She skirted the bonfire in her favorite faded black Seven jeans and the long-sleeved black Marc by Marc Jacobs scoop-neck she'd found scouring the clearance racks at Barneys. It was a pretty top, made from the softest cotton imaginable, with a lace-trimmed neckline. Unfortunately it was entirely hidden by the silly orange Usual Suspects T-shirt she'd pulled tight over the top. She felt ridiculous, but everyone else on the dean's suspect list was wearing the shirt, and she didn't want anyone to think she thought she was above suspicion.

She kept one eye on her roommate at all times, rotating around the crater as Callie made her way through the crowd, in order to not run into her. They'd been avoiding each other in their room, too, which was relatively easy now that Callie spent all her free time with Easy. Jenny filled a plastic cup from the newly refreshed tub of Jungle Juice. She pressed her fingers into her alabaster skin, rubbing her arms to ward off a chill brought on by the dropping temperature and by the ice-cold cup in her hand.

"Cold?"

Jenny whipped around, catching a tendril of curly brown hair in her eye. She'd hoped to find Julian standing next to her. Instead, it was Easy Walsh, who hadn't said a word to her since he'd broken up with her last week. She'd seen him around since then, of course, but it was fairly clear that he'd been avoiding her. She took a sip from her plastic cup and held it to her lips longer than necessary, waiting for him to state his business or walk away.

"Heath's outdone himself again, huh?" Easy's dark blue eyes scanned her face nervously. It was nice to see him nervous. She'd never had the upper hand in anything, and she was determined not to give in to Easy Walsh the way everyone else did. Even though he did look kind of adorable in his orange US shirt, which was already grass-stained. From what? Rolling around in the woods with Callie?

"The bonfire was a bold touch, I'll give him that," Jenny answered, scanning the crowd for people she actually wanted to talk to. Brandon was over by the fire, but his head was turned toward Sage Francis and they seemed to be deep in conversation. Brett hadn't arrived yet, and Kara was lying on the ground, staring up at the stars through the opening in the treetops—with Heath. That was a little random. Alison was kneeling in front of the fire with Alan right behind her, toasting a marshmallow on a long stick. It looked like Julian hadn't arrived, either. There, Jenny thought, that was the extent of the people she wanted to talk to. Six weeks at Waverly and she could count her friends on one hand. And she'd thought she was doing so well.

"I was hoping I'd see you here," Easy said, his voice sounding a bit strange.

Jenny couldn't help but wonder what he meant by that. *Why, so you can humiliate me again? So you can pretend to like me until your ex-girlfriend comes back? So you can blame me for the fire?*

She decided against them all, punctuating the silence with a simple, "Oh?"

Easy pawed at the ground with his already-filthy, on-the-verge-of-disintegrating brown Camper bowling shoes. He scratched the back of his neck, the growing bonfire reflected in his dark blue eyes.

"Anyway, I wanted to tell you that I'm sorry about everything." He bent over and picked up a long stick from the ground, trying to twirl it in his fingers.

Jenny turned to face him for the first time.

"I never, uh, *wanted* to hurt you." He dropped the stick abruptly and ran his hand over his face. He lowered his voice so that Jenny had to lean in a little closer to hear him. "And I really didn't want you to find out about me and Callie . . . like that," he went on, his face flushing, probably at the memory of the two of them fleeing the burning barn half naked in front of the whole campus. "I'm sure that was really terrible for you. I can't imagine. . . ." He struggled to complete his sentence, bailing himself out with a swig of Jungle Juice from his red Solo cup.

"Yeah, well." The apology meant a lot to Jenny, but she couldn't fully absorb it with the mayhem around them. Ryan Reynolds brushed past, chasing a sophomore girl in a short skirt and shouting, "I'm a suspect, too! They just forgot to get me a shirt!"

"And I know Callie is being a total pain in the ass right now," Easy added, lowering his voice a little. "With the fire and all." He coughed, still speaking quietly. "She is totally paranoid that uh, you got us on the list, to uh, cover the fact that you actually started the fire."

Jenny stood there quietly, smoldering.

"I didn't realize how stupid that sounded until I said it out loud. I know you'd never do anything like that." Easy looked at her, and for the first time since they started talking, Jenny met his gaze. She could tell he really did think Callie's theory was nuts, which made her feel a bit better. He swallowed, his Adam's apple bobbing up and down. "God, this is all so fucked up."

Jenny felt the cloud of the last few days lifting. If Easy was on her side, maybe things would turn out all right in the end after all. "Thanks for . . . telling me all this," she said. It struck her how much she missed talking to him. Easy was the kind of guy you just wanted on your team. "That really means a lot."

Callie glared at Easy and Jenny from across the bonfire, unsure whether it was the heat from the flames or the sight of them together, speaking so earnestly, that made her face burn. All she could think about was how just a few weeks ago Easy had dumped her for that little slut. There was no doubt at all in her mind: Jenny had to go.

She poured the remainder of her cup of Jungle Juice out

carelessly on the ground, her head already buzzing from the alcohol. Then she scanned the party, looking for the one person whose presence would comfort her. Her eyes finally landed on Tinsley. Her dark-haired friend was standing with Chloe by one of the punch bowls of Jungle Juice, handing the girl an over-flowing cup. Callie smiled and headed in that direction. Tinsley would be happy to know she was back on board, ready to get Jenny kicked out once and for all.

A WAVERLY OWL DOES NOT ENGAGE IN
UNDERAGE DRINKING.

"Name?"

Brett jumped, not realizing she'd almost stepped on Sam, who stood guard over the scene behind him, holding a clipboard. She noticed a few orange T-shirts emblazoned with US in black letters across the front and USUAL SUSPECT across the back—she spotted Brandon in one, and Benny. Sam's was the same color as the others', but the letters DM were painted on the front. Huh? What did that stand for? Sam turned to harass two sophomores not on the guest list. Brett read the words DEFLOWER ME on the back. She rolled her eyes.

"Here's your T-shirt," he told her flatly, turning back to Brett and handing her a plastic bag with the party T-shirt inside. "You can change in the tent." He paused. "Or you can just change right here."

Brett rolled her eyes again as someone she vaguely recognized from first-period Latin stumbled by and handed her a red-and-orange drink. She immediately flashed back to her awful first party at Waverly, which was also at the Crater. That night, she drank three Tequila Sunrises without realizing they were full of tequila, and spent the rest of the night hugging a tree trunk. She sniffed the contents of the plastic cup and a strong odor of vodka filled her nose. She took a sip and tasted the familiar tang of Jungle Juice, one of Heath's favorite elixirs.

Brett scanned the party, hoping to find Kara's familiar head of brown hair. She really wanted to apologize for her moody fit earlier today, but she couldn't make Kara out in the mass of bodies gathered around the flickering light of the bonfire. Verena Arneval was getting into the now-or-never spirit with a sophomore on the tennis team. The two seemed to be dancing to music only they could hear, grinding precariously close to the fire. A little way off, Benny was sitting cross-legged on the grassy knoll with Lon Baruzza. He was a scholarship student and rumored to be great in bed. Lon massaged Benny's back, presumably giving her a preview of his moves. Brett spotted Jenny's familiar head of curls and was about to head in her direction, but stopped herself when she realized she was deep in conversation with Easy, of all people. What was that about? Brett didn't see Heath anywhere, which was a bit strange—but then, he'd probably drunk too much and was already passed out in the woods.

Brett felt a strong hand on her bare arm and whirled around.

Was Ryan Reynolds manhandling her again? Instead, a defense-less Jeremiah put up his hands in surrender.

"Whoa, whoa!" he said, stepping backward. Wearing his black James Perse polo over his favorite red thermal shirt and his old faded green J.Crew cargo pants, he looked startlingly familiar. He'd trimmed his red hair since the last time she'd seen him, at the disastrous Dumbarton party two weeks ago. It was much less shaggy than she was used to, although he'd let a little stubble grow on his cheeks and chin, which made his angular, square jaw look even more defined. "I'm inno-cent, I swear." Despite being from an old-money family in Newton, a suburb of Boston, Jeremiah spoke with a Boston accent, and the word came out *sway-ah*. When they were dating, his townie accent had always bothered Brett, but now it just sounded cute.

"Jeremiah!" Brett stood on her tiptoes and kissed him on both stubbly cheeks. He smelled woodsy and clean. It was good to see him. "What are you *doing* here?" Even though St. Lucius people regularly turned out for Waverly parties, it was a Tuesday night, and she knew Jeremiah had a big game this weekend—he was the football team's star lineman—so she had thought it unlikely that he'd make it out for this. If she'd known he'd be here, she would have made sure to reply to his e-mail—she felt bad now that she'd ignored it, too overwhelmed by the fire and the Kara situation to figure out what to say.

Jeremiah blushed. She smiled when she remembered how easily she could make him blush. "I heard about the hearing or whatever tomorrow and, well, in case it was your last night . . ."

He peered down at her, his hands still lingering on her waist after their hug. "I wanted to make sure to say goodbye."

"You're so sweet." Brett looked up into his blue-green eyes and felt a weird sensation in her stomach. It must have been the Jungle Juice kicking in. She raised her plastic cup to her lips, still smiling at Jeremiah. She felt so . . . liberated. The whole scene of total irreverence—the fact that everyone was making fun of the fire situation, even embracing how insane it all was—felt a heck of a lot better than whispering about it behind each others' backs and making accusations. She hadn't put on her goony T-shirt yet—she was wearing a pretty sheer black peasant shirt, borrowed from Jenny, and she didn't want to cover it up—but when she spotted Alison Quentin wearing her eight-sizes-too-big US shirt, she decided it actually looked pretty cute. So why not get into the spirit of the thing? She handed her cup to Jeremiah. "Hold this?"

"Anything for you, B." He grinned, exposing his row of adorably crooked bottom teeth, and took the cup from her. His huge, strong hands dwarfed the red plastic cup. Brett pulled her shirt on over her head, stumbling a little. The vodka in her drink had already messed with her balance.

Jeremiah took a swig of Brett's drink and then made a disgusted face, spitting it out on the ground.

"Hey!" she chastised, swatting his arm. "I was going to drink that!"

"Just thought I'd give it a try." He laughed, wiping his mouth with his sleeve. "How you drink that stuff I'll never understand." Jeremiah was a notorious beer-drinker and always teased Brett about her love of cocktails and mixed drinks. She suddenly remembered how during their first week back at school, he'd invited her on a trip to wine country with his family—his dad was opening up a new restaurant and was headed to Sonoma on a tasting tour over Thanksgiving. At the time, she'd been totally unenthusiastic. She was entranced by the sophisticated Eric Dalton and had imagined Jeremiah chugging the wine instead of sipping it at all the vineyards. God, she'd been so unfair to him. She hoped he'd forgiven her, or that if he hadn't, he would soon.

"Let's get you a beer." Impulsively, she grabbed his hand and headed toward the woods, where the kegs were usually kept at Crater parties. His fingers were like old friends she hadn't seen in forever.

"Are you nervous?" Jeremiah asked as they walked. Branches crackled beneath their feet, and the woods smelled piney and romantic. The noise receded as they drew away from the crowd. "About tomorrow, I mean. Jesus, the whole thing is so wack."

Brett was glad that it was dark so Jeremiah couldn't see her blushing. When he'd asked if she was nervous, she'd automatically thought about the last time he asked her that question—on the night they had planned to lose their virginity to each other.

But before she could answer they both stopped short, suddenly aware of a rustling in the grass. Brett squinted, expecting an owl to flap up from the ground, but was drawn instead to two figures in the tall grass just ahead. She put a finger to her lips and Jeremiah nodded, an embarrassed smile spreading across his face.

"Whoops," he mouthed.

Brett's eyes adjusted to the moonlight. She could just make out the faces of the two figures sitting cross-legged in the grass, heads bent together, whispering intimately. She froze, staring. What was *Heath* doing sitting in the woods alone with a girl, *just talking*? His Mini Me, Sam, would have been disappointed. She was about to turn away when the moonlight caught the girl's face. It was Kara.

Brett kept on staring as Heath took his hand, placed it under Kara's chin, and lifted it up toward his face. Then he kissed her, their lips moving softly against each other. Brett stood frozen in astonishment.

"Yo, where's the keg?"

She whipped her head around to see Benny standing behind her, giggling, Lon Baruzza's arms wrapped around her tiny waist. Benny shook her empty cup at Brett for emphasis. But then she spotted Heath and Kara, and her eyes widened. "Oh shit," she said, looking at Brett in confusion. Brett wished she'd keep her voice down—Heath and Kara hadn't noticed they were there, and she didn't want them to. "Why's your girlfriend kissing Heath?!" Benny exclaimed loudly.

Jeremiah dropped Brett's hand. He turned to her, his blue-green eyes filled with confusion and hurt. "*Girlfriend*? So what I heard is really *true*?"

Brett stood there, completely mute, wishing the bonfire would burn the woods down. She'd rather run for her life from another fire than defend herself—from what? What had she done? Obviously she didn't have a girlfriend if her supposed girlfriend was currently in a liplock with Heath Ferro. She grasped her cup tightly in her hand and stumbled back toward the bonfire. "I think I need another drink."

A CONSIDERATE OWL APPRECIATES YOUNG LOVE.

Brandon could feel Sage's breath on his face, they were that close. He held the edge of his plastic cup between his teeth, his hands ceremonially out of the way as he tilted the cup toward the night sky and took a sip of Jungle Juice. Sage giggled as a river of the alcohol ran down his cheek, and he smiled as much as he could without dropping the cup. "Okay," he mumbled through his teeth. "Now you."

Sage leaned in and bit down on the plastic cup. Brandon had never noticed how blue her eyes were—like the sky at the Cape on one of those endless July afternoons—or how perfectly smooth her skin was.

"Got it?" he asked through clenched teeth.

"Got it," she answered back, her eyes wide and framed with a smudgy dark blue liner. Maybe that's why they were so bright.

Brandon pulled back. "No cheating now." He grinned wickedly as she tilted the cup back. He watched her neck as she swallowed a huge gulp of the orangish concoction. She let out a high-pitched squeal and jolted forward. Some of the Jungle Juice spilled back out of her mouth and into the cup.

"Oh, that's just gross," he teased her. He was pleasantly buzzed by this time and couldn't help taking a peek at Sage's chest, hugged tightly in her orange US shirt.

"Lemme try." Sam appeared suddenly in front of them.

"Let's see some ID." Brandon crossed his arms in front of his chest. It was fun acting all tough in front of the prospectives. He could get used to it.

"No, really. C'mon." Sam reached for the cup, but Sage whisked it out of his reach, holding it up over her head so that a strip of bare skin appeared between her jeans and her T-shirt. Sam picked at the DM decal on the front of his T-shirt. "This shirt itches," he said to no one in particular.

"Take it off," Brandon suggested.

"I can't. Not yet," Sam said seriously.

"Why not?" Sage asked curiously. She shook her head, her long corn silk hair shivering in long waves.

"Because it hasn't happened yet," Sam said plainly, as if the answer were obvious. He scanned the crowd and ran a hand over his artfully gelled hair, the gesture looking particularly Heath-like. "Have you seen Heath? He was supposed to hook me up tonight. He promised."

Brandon glanced around at the party, having sort of forgotten where he was. He'd been sitting by the fire with Sage, talking about movies. She had pretty terrible taste, but at least she knew it, and let him tease her about her love for *Coyote Ugly* and *Legally Blonde*. "They're girl power movies," she'd explained. Sage was astonishingly unpretentious and easy to talk to. Her bottom front teeth were slightly crooked, which only seemed to make the rest of her face seem perfect. "Haven't seen him," Brandon shrugged, dragging his eyes back to Sam. "He's probably passed out in the bushes."

Sam looked alarmed, as if Brandon had told him his parents had just died in a car crash. "No way, dude." He looked at Sage lustily and turned to Brandon, lowering his voice a little. "Can *you* hook me up?" He cocked his head toward Sage, who pressed her hands over her pale pink lips to stifle a laugh.

"Sorry, man," Brandon said, hoping that would be the end of it. Sam seemed to gravitate toward him whenever Heath wasn't around, and Brandon was getting sick of it. He knew he'd have to make a halfhearted attempt to look for Heath if he wanted more alone time with Sage.

"Stay right here," Brandon instructed Sam, "and we'll send him over. Don't move."

"Okay, but hurry," Sam said, plopping down on a log bench nearby. He glanced at his oversize plastic watch.

"We will," Brandon said solemnly. He reached for Sage's hand, which was warm to his touch, and pulled her away, steering her through the crowd of drunken revelers. He didn't mind looking for Heath, but he wanted to be alone with Sage while he did it.

"Poor kid," Sage observed. It was exciting to have her warm

hand in his, though Brandon wondered if he should drop it soon.

"He's better off," Brandon assured her. "Heath's been filling his head with crap about how he got laid when he was a prospective." Normally he never would've said "got laid" in front of a girl, especially not one he was trying to charm, but the words escaped before he could stop them.

"Gross," Sage responded. Brandon didn't know if she was turned off by Heath, or by his language. But she didn't drop his hand, so he took that as a good sign.

"And I have to room with him," Brandon joked.

"Just as long as his bad habits don't rub off on you," Sage said, glancing sideways at him.

They ducked into one of the tents and Brandon looked around, hoping to spot Heath's familiar head of dirty-blond hair. But there were only Erik Olssen and Tricia Rieken, that Swedish guy and the girl who'd had a boob job, their faces pressed together and their clothes disheveled. They turned to glare at Brandon and Sage.

"Sorry." Brandon grabbed Sage's hand and led her back outside the tent as they stifled their giggles. But they began to laugh even harder when they saw what was going on ten yards away.

Apparently, Sam hadn't waited for them to get back. He was on his knees at Chloe's feet, staring up at her with a clump of wildflowers and weeds, clearly just pulled from the ground somewhere, in his outstretched hands. "But you're so *beautiful!*" Sam slurred up at her. "I just want to cuddle."

"Ohmigod, that is totally Heath's work," Sage giggled. "But it's also kind of cute, in a demented sort of way."

"C'mon," Brandon whispered, electrified by the way Sage's small fingers seemed to fit so perfectly in his. They turned back toward the roaring party. Sage squeezed his hand and a delirium he hadn't felt in forever spread through him, leaping and darting like the dying bonfire.

22

A WAVERLY OWL KNOWS THAT SOMETIMES THE TRUTH HURTS.

Jenny searched the growing crowd, the Jungle Juice tickling her brain. The party was beginning to look like a raging fire itself: a shifting mass of red- and yellow-clad bodies, the occasional orange US shirt visible, with the flames from the bonfire flickering all over the scene. She couldn't wait to see Julian and was feeling better than she had all week. Easy had apologized. A kiss from Julian would complete her night.

Then she spotted him, heading in the direction of a group of squash guys. His longish hair was freshly washed and tucked behind his ears. He wore a baby-blue Adidas track jacket with yellow stripes over his US shirt, something Heath probably would not have approved of. Not that Heath was anywhere to be seen.

She waved to him and he smiled and started toward her, his long legs taking him quickly to her side. He stepped on a cinder that leaped from the bonfire, smothering it into the grass until it was reduced to smoke. "That's all we need, right?"

"Right." Jenny smiled. She waited as he dipped himself a cup of Jungle Juice and joined her on the edge of the crater.

"Maybe we should go, um, check out the woods?" Julian asked. The flames of the fire lit up his face, and his cute once-broken nose stood out from the shadows. Jenny wished she could lean forward and kiss it. The woods? Did he want to hook up with her right away?

"Could we hang here for a bit first?" Not that she wasn't excited by the idea, but she'd been looking forward to hanging out for a while and being all coupley in front of everyone. She sat down on one of the logs. It was hard to talk to Julian when they were both standing up, since he was a million feet taller than she was. It made her neck hurt.

"Yeah, of course." Julian sat down next to her on the log, but then he looked behind him in both directions, as if to make sure they weren't being watched. "Actually, I don't really feel like Jungle Juice. I heard there was beer in one of the tents. Help me look?" He stood up again abruptly, and Jenny couldn't help but wonder why he was so jumpy all of a sudden.

"Sure, no problem," Jenny got up, too, and they started walking. "Chloe's totally in love with you, by the way," she couldn't resist pointing out. After they'd left Julian at the steps of his dorm, he was all Chloe had been able to talk about.

"Yeah?" Julian looked genuinely surprised, and Jenny loved that he had no idea how charming he was. "Too bad I like my girls a little older." He raised his eyebrows suggestively, although Jenny thought she detected a trace of nervousness in his voice.

Benny ran by at full speed, screaming in delight as Lon Baruzza chased after her. They knocked over a castle of empty plastic cups constructed by two freshmen who sat dangerously close to the fire. One of the plastic cups fell into the fire and started smoldering, polluting the immediate vicinity with the rancid smell of burning plastic.

Julian led the way and they searched several tents, interrupting couples in various states of undress before they found the last four cans of Budweiser in an empty tent with different-size lava lamps in it.

"There must be kegs somewhere," Julian noted, pulling the sleeves of his track jacket down over his hands to handle the ice-cold beers, which had been sitting in a small cooler.

Jenny nodded. Waverly's male population couldn't *all* be drinking Jungle Juice. She had a feeling Heath had prepared the concoction not out of love for super-sweet mixed drinks, but because it got girls drunk quickly. "Too bad I'm new and you're a freshman. We don't know the insider keg secrets yet," she said with a smile. She kind of liked that they were both newbies at Waverly. Everybody else here seemed to have such tangled pasts and dark histories. But being with Julian felt like a fresh start.

"Too true. But no worries, these'll do." Julian smiled, the dimple to the left of his mouth appearing for a moment. He slipped a can from the plastic ring and offered one to Jenny, but she shook her head, and they sat down on the hard ground.

There was a noise outside the tent and Julian nearly jumped, looking over his shoulder.

"You're nervous about tomorrow, aren't you?" Jenny asked, her forehead wrinkling in concern. She was glad she'd figured out the source of his unease. For all his talk of having a cute girlfriend for an alibi, he had to be totally freaked out about the dean's meeting tomorrow. After all, he had no way of proving he had lost his lighter.

"Yeah," Julian nodded. His eyes were distant, and the lights from all the lava lamps cast sinister-looking shadows on their faces.

"So . . ." Jenny picked up the plastic web that had held the beer cans and thrust her tiny wrist through one of the circles, wearing it like a bracelet. "What *are* you going to say when they ask about your lighter?"

He took a long swig of his beer and then set it down on the ground in front of him. He shrugged. "I'm going to tell them the truth."

"Which is?" Jenny had a sudden gnawing feeling in her stomach.

"Why don't you tell *her* the truth. About *everything?*" Tinsley suddenly appeared behind them, wearing a pair of slim-fitting black L.A.M.B. pants and a supertight black Ogle turtleneck. She towered over Jenny, her slim figure perfectly silhouetted against the white backdrop of the tent, and the space felt suddenly suffocating. The red light from the lava lamps played over her features, making her look positively devilish.

The hairs on Jenny's neck prickled in warning. "What's she

talking about?" she demanded. Julian was staring up at Tinsley, an angry look on his face. What was going on?

Tinsley watched as Jenny's annoyingly cherubic face wrinkled in worry. She knew it probably would have been smarter to keep Jenny in the dark about her and Julian. But when she'd spotted them ducking into the tent from across the party, looking all cute and coupley, Tinsley was reminded, as though by a slap in the face, that she'd been unceremoniously thrown over by a *freshman*. And for that big-chested dwarf, no less. At least her reign of over-boobed terror was about to come to an end, once and for all.

"Julian?" Jenny asked again, looking up at him fearfully.

"Tell her," Tinsley said again, placing her hands on her hips in challenge. Julian frowned at her in annoyance, and she felt a momentary stir of regret—or maybe it was just pity. But really—did he think he could just dump Tinsley Carmichael and not suffer the consequences?

He sloshed back a mouthful of beer, as if to fortify himself, and then turned to Jenny. "I . . . I . . . Tinsley and I . . ."

He didn't have to say anything else. Those two words— *Tinsley and I*—were all she needed to hear. They seared Jenny in half, tattooing themselves on her heart. She resisted the urge to hit him, but just barely. She couldn't really slap him in disgust like girlfriends and wives did on TV—because she wasn't really his girlfriend, and she never had been.

"That's why you were always outside Dumbarton. . . ." She started to put the pieces together. He hadn't been there to try to see her. He'd been there because he was hooking up with

Tinsley. That was why he'd wanted to go off campus, too, and why he'd been so jumpy tonight—he was afraid Tinsley might see them. She wasn't sure what hurt her more: that he'd been hooking up with the gorgeous mega-bitch who loomed over her at this very instant, or that he'd *lied* to her.

"But it was all *before* you," Julian insisted. "Before I really met you." He was looking at her intently, his brown eyes pleading, but she felt as though she didn't recognize him anymore. He was just a tall figure with shaggy hair, a faceless boy she'd never really even known.

She stood up, shook off Julian's hand, and wandered away from him, and Tinsley, and the party, and everyone in it. How could she have been so clueless—again? And what was she doing in a place full of liars and jerks?

From: HeathFerro@waverly.edu
To: Undisclosed Recipients
Date: Tuesday, October 15, 11:52 P.M.
Subject: Go US, go US, go go go US

My dear US's and other less fortunates,

Thank you, ladies and gents, for giving US such a fan-fucking-tabulous farewell party.

I hope you're all still as drunk as I am.

Thanks for not burning the Crater down. It's all we've got.

Xxx

Heath

A WAVERLY OWL ARRIVES PROMPTLY FOR
DISCIPLINARY APPOINTMENTS.

Brett could tell by Mr. Tomkins's solemn glare that she was late. *Oops.* At breakfast she'd been jittery and had spilled an entire cup of coffee on her previously cream-colored Diane von Furstenberg wool skirt, a hand-me-down from her older sister, Bree. She'd had to dash back to Dumbarton, toss on the pair of jeans draped over her desk chair, and fly over to Stansfield Hall, out of breath and probably totally guilty-looking. The door to Dean Marymount's office was left ajar and Brett could see the back of Callie's head, her strawberry blond hair pulled back into a perfectly neat ponytail. The dead silence inside the office filled her with dread.

"Go on." Mr. Tomkins nodded for her to go inside, and she slipped through the door to find that she was, in fact, the last of the Usual Suspects to arrive. Heath looked up from his chair at the end of the enormous oak conference table under the window, registered Brett's presence with a nod, and then lowered his head back into his hands. A quick look around the room revealed similar reactions: Tinsley's hooded eyes were barely open; Callie looked like she hadn't slept all night. Jenny, wearing a pink button-down shirt beneath her Waverly blazer, held a cup of coffee from Maxwell, her knuckles white. Easy yawned silently three times in a row, until Callie nudged him with her elbow to stop. Alison Quentin, wearing a navy blue Polo turtleneck, was rubbing her left temple vigorously, as if trying to work out a kink. Even Brandon, who normally didn't leave his dorm room without looking his best, seemed to have fallen asleep sitting up. Next to him Sage whispered to Benny behind two tall energy smoothies. Only Julian seemed to not be hungover. He stared out the window at the red and gold leaves shimmering in the morning light with unfathomable serenity.

Brett herself was a total mess. She hadn't slept at all last night. As she'd tossed and turned, she'd tried to figure out which bothered her more: the image of Kara kissing Heath, or the look on Jeremiah's face when he'd found out she had a girlfriend. Did that mean she was straight after all? Did she still have feelings for Jeremiah? Her mind was such a mess of conflicting thoughts, she wondered if she'd ever untangle them.

Jenny raised her eyebrows in Brett's direction and looked like she was about to say something, but instead she took a small sip of her coffee—under Tinsley's watchful eye. Tinsley's gaze roamed from Jenny to Callie to Julian, before landing momentarily on Brett. "Those my jeans, roomie?" she asked, somewhat cheerfully, shattering the awkward silence in the room and causing everyone to look up. Brett glanced down at the jeans she had grabbed from the chair—her chair—that morning. She'd thought they were her dark-rinse Paige jeans and had been too preoccupied with running across campus to notice that they fit a little differently than she was used to. Fuck.

"Didn't think you'd mind," Brett threw back, her voice dripping with sweetness, "since you left them on my desk chair."

Tinsley grinned back at her. "What are roommates for?" She wore an emerald Rebecca Beeson crew-neck dress, and her long black hair was parted neatly in the middle, falling down over her ears like curtains of silk. Brett took pleasure in the fact that although Tinsley's hair looked perfect, her face looked haggard and hungover.

Not that Brett had gotten her beauty sleep, either. It was hard to believe that this time tomorrow, one of them would be gone, like they'd never even been at Waverly in the first place.

She remembered a girl from her freshman year—Sylvia something or other. One day everyone woke up and Sylvia had just vanished, expelled for plagiarizing an English paper. Brett's first thought when she heard about Sylvia's expulsion was a selfish one—the girl had borrowed a Wilco CD. Brett stayed angry about the CD for more than a week, until she replaced it at Trax-n-Wax in town. She mentally ran through the list of Usual Suspects, trying to remember if she had any outstanding debts—lunch money borrowed, clothes unreturned, anything at all that might malign her memory if Dean Marymount marched her to the tall iron front gates and gave her the boot.

As far as she knew, her accounts had all been settled. But maybe she'd manage to not give Tinsley back her fucking jeans.

Dean Marymount strode in, whistling a tune Brett couldn't place. He looked well rested, his clean-shaven face rosy in the morning light. If he knew anything about the goodbye party the night before, his face betrayed no hint of it. How could he not have smelled the bonfire smoke? Was the smoke from the weekend's barn fire still masking it, as Heath claimed? "Hello, Owls," he greeted them.

Everyone seated around the room nodded silently, except Tinsley, who trained her violet eyes on Marymount, unafraid to meet his gaze.

"I've made a decision of great interest to everyone in this room," Marymount announced grandly, as if he were going to tell one of them they'd just won a new car, or a trip for two to Hawaii. Brett's heart skipped a beat. Was he going to let them all go? He straightened the calendar on his desk so that it made a perfect ninety-degree angle with the square pencil holder as the room waited in anxious silence. "Rather than try to ferret out the guilty party or parties with respect to the fire at the Miller farm, I'm going to let you work it out among yourselves."

What? A murmur went around the room. Brett gauged the faces of her fellow inmates. Everyone had been planning to back each other's stories against Marymount. But suddenly they had to defend themselves against *one another?*

"Quiet." Marymount's cheerful expression soured. "So here's how it's going to work. I'm going to breakfast with the prospectives, whom I hope you've all been treating with great sensitivity and respect. When I come back, I'll hear a confession from the guilty party. Whoever steps forward and says, 'I did it,' will be expelled, of course, and the rest of you will be free to go about your day. How does that sound?" He didn't wait for a response. "Mr. Tomkins will be outside the door. If you need something, he'll attend to you. But please don't waste his time or yours with stall tactics. This ends here and now. Any questions?" He glanced quickly around the room and turned toward the door, clearly not expecting anyone to take issue with this change of events.

Brett cleared her throat. If the junior class prefect couldn't speak up, what the hell was the point of being one? "But, sir." Her voice came out as a squeak, so she cleared her throat again. "What if the real culprits aren't here?"

Marymount looked at her evenly through his round, gold-rimmed glasses. Wearing his favorite blue crew-neck sweater beneath his Waverly blazer, he looked ready to give a lecture on *The Tempest,* not to ruin some poor student's life. "They are," he said simply, leaving no room for debate. "Any other questions?" He knit his sandy gray bushy eyebrows.

There were none.

"Excellent." Marymount gathered some papers from his desk. Then he pulled out his chair and invited Brett to have a seat. "No use standing, Ms. Messerschmidt. This could take awhile."

Brett didn't know if she was being set up, but she took a seat anyway, her tired legs almost collapsing under her as she sat in his high-backed leather chair, in full view of her class-mates at the large oval table.

"Oh, I forgot." Marymount paused in the doorway, the framed Waverly class graduation photos behind him. In them, the smiling, rosy-cheeked graduates held their Waverly diplomas aloft gleefully, seeming to mock the students in the room. "If by the time I've returned you haven't uncovered the guilty party among you, you'll *all* be expelled."

Brett had never seen so many jaws drop at once before.

Dean Marymount continued. "So think long and hard about it. I urge you to take this seriously. That includes you, Mr. Ferro." And with that, he was gone.

Heath flipped Marymount off as the door closed, but no one laughed.

Tinsley was the first to speak in Marymount's wake. "It's fucking boiling in here." She went to the window and heaved it open, the cool morning air swirling into the musty office. Everyone took deep, gulping breaths, as if they hadn't inhaled since the dean's announcement.

"Is he kidding?" Callie demanded, looking at no one in particular. She'd worn a puffy white cashmere sweater that looked like a remnant from middle school, and a blue-and-white-striped jersey dress, obviously trying to look as responsible and innocent as possible.

"Where's Kara?" Heath asked suddenly, startling everyone. He ran a hand through his shaggy dirty-blond hair, looking like he wanted to go back to bed.

Brett searched the room and realized, along with everyone else, that Kara had skipped the morning meeting. Her green eyes widened.

"Funny, Marymount didn't say anything," Jenny said, her small voice sounding out of place in the stark room. She looked tiny compared to the high-backed leather chair she sat in.

"I say *she* did it." Benny sat up straighter, clapping her hands together. Her brown hair was in a braid at the nape of her neck, and tiny Tiffany diamond studs sparkled in either ear. "Case closed. Somebody grab the dean."

Brett felt her body tense, as if everyone was looking at her, expecting a reaction.

But Heath spoke up first in Kara's defense. "Come on." Heath tried to save his outburst by cracking a smile, but Brett noticed everyone shooting him a curious look. "She's probably just too hungover." He was still wearing his orange US shirt, which was heavily wrinkled, as though he'd slept in it—or hadn't gone to bed at all. Had he been up all night with Kara? Brett shook her red hair out of her face, trying to banish the thought. It was a good thing Heath's back was facing the wall—otherwise the dean would have seen the USUAL SUSPECTS written across the back of his shirt. They were in enough trouble as it was without Marymount knowing they'd had an enormous party making fun of him and his list.

"What if we all staged a protest?" Sage threw out, tapping her peach-colored nails against the oak table. "I'm sure if we all told Marymount we were leaving campus until this . . . persecution stops, he'd have to back off, right?" She looked around the room and finally let her gaze rest on Brandon, who sat in the chair next to her.

"It won't work," Brandon said in a flat voice. He was sitting awfully close to Sage, and Brett wondered if the intimate conversation she'd spotted them having last night had gone anywhere. The light played off Brandon's golden head of hair, and Brett couldn't help but hope something *had* happened between them. Brandon was so cute, he deserved a girl who wasn't going to screw him over the way Callie and that St. Lucius ho-bag, Elizabeth, had. She immediately thought of Jeremiah—she still couldn't believe he'd slept with that Elizabeth girl, even if it was a rebound hookup after being dumped by Brett. But after facing a dangerous fire, in a room full of people facing expulsion, Jeremiah's indiscretion suddenly didn't seem like such a big deal anymore.

Brandon shrugged. "Marymount wants someone to take the fall, and he's not going to give a shit who it is."

"Look, someone started the fire, either by accident, or . . ." Brett's voice trailed off. "But, whoever you are, are you really willing to let everyone else take the fall for you?"

"Yeah, dude, that's not cool." Heath propped his black leather Adidas on the smooth oak table. No one else spoke.

Outside, a burst of laughter filtered in from the quad, and everyone gazed longingly toward the windows. Easy put his head down on the table and a couple of others followed suit. The room fell silent again. What felt like an eternity passed as all the Usual Suspects sat in stony, contemplative silence.

"Oh my God." The words escaped Brett's lips automatically, her brain and mouth working simultaneously. She'd cast her eyes down on Marymount's desk to try and keep her focus, and she had to look twice at the family picture perched behind a pencil holder stuffed full of sharpened number twos and the gigantic stapler with the ominous DO NOT REMOVE sticker across the head. She reached for the silver frame, bringing it close to her nose for inspection. She could hardly believe it. Marymount's wife, the only other person Brett thought she recognized, was smiling at him as if he'd just said something really funny. It was a normal photo of a cheesy family get-together, one that could probably be found on countless desks of Waverly teachers. But Brett recognized someone else in the photo. She stood up and strode over to the closest person, who happened to be Sage, and handed it to her for verification.

"You've got to be fucking kidding me." Sage's glossy lips dropped open. She held up the family photo for everyone to see, the fluttery sleeve of her pink Splendid blouse sliding up her arm.

"What?" Alison asked, raising her head from the table and looking up at Brett. One of the pink plastic butterfly barrettes holding back her smooth black hair had slid out of place.

"It's Chloe," Brett answered, her voice emptied of all emotion. "That little sneak."

"*What's* Chloe?" Alison asked, panicked.

"She's *related* to him?" Benny's voice rose, incredulous. She stood up.

"Who?" Brandon asked, rubbing his eyes with his fists. "What's going on?"

"I asked her if anyone in her family had ever gone to Waverly, and she mentioned something about her uncle. She could've fucking told us he was the dean." Benny shook her head, frustrated, and her long braid of shiny brown hair flopped from side to side. But then she gasped loudly, covering her mouth with her manicured hand. "I told her about the stash of booze in our room."

Sage turned to look at her roommate. "And she was totally interrogating me about what Easy and Callie were doing in the stables on Saturday." Callie blushed, and Easy squeezed her hand under the table.

"But that means," Alison started, then stopped, staring at the ceiling as if she was trying to work out a difficult algebra problem in her head. "She said this weird thing to me about Alan helping me *study*," she said. "It didn't register at the time, but . . ." She scrunched up her face. "Little bitch."

Tinsley smirked and leaned back in her leather chair so far that Brett hoped it would topple to the floor. She stacked her black leather Sigerson Morrison heels on the table. "Wow, that's underhanded. You've got to kind of admire it."

Understanding washed over Heath's face. "I was only kidding about the naked rule. . . ." Brandon's eyes narrowed at his roommate, and Heath put both hands up, as if to proclaim his innocence. "So basically, we're all in here because we said or did compromising things in front of that little prospective?" he cried, glancing around the room. He looked like he was both indignant and impressed.

"Yeah, or because we were mean to her. And then she ran and told her uncle. It's so freaking *unfair*." Alison grabbed a piece of her hair and started nibbling on the ends angrily.

"I'll tell you what's unfair," Benny said suddenly, shushing the room. She clicked her pointy nails against the countertop. "Kara's probably sleeping off her hangover somewhere, while we're all trying to decide who gets kicked out of school."

Brett winced at the mention of Kara's name. She wasn't sure if it would be better or worse if Kara were actually here. Why had she skipped the meeting? It was probably in protest—Kara was the one person gutsy enough to actually do something like that.

Heath spoke up again, this time a bit more forcefully. "I told you, cut her some slack. She just had a late night is all."

Benny shrugged her shoulders. "Heathie, I know you're feeling guilty because you got her drunk so you could make out with her or whatever, but honestly, we were all up as late as you two and *we* all still made it here." Benny stuck out her tongue at Heath and then realized what she'd blurted and turned to Brett with an apologetic look.

Brett felt the whole room staring at her. She was tired of shrinking from her classmates' gazes and sat up straighter in the dean's high-backed chair. "We saw you, in the woods," she said evenly, swiveling the chair slightly to gaze right at Heath. She hoped no one asked who "we" included—no need to drag Jeremiah into this.

Heath's handsome face turned a shade pinker. "Brett—I, uh . . . can we go somewhere and talk?"

Brett shook her head, her gaze still locked on Heath. "You can say whatever you need to say right here. There are no secrets at Waverly, right?" She crossed her arms over her chest and looked around the table at her classmates, narrowing her green eyes. Everyone looked away or put their heads down on the table, as if they were trying to fade into the background. Yeah, right. They all wanted to hear the dirty details. Jenny, at least, met her gaze and gave her a sympathetic look with her warm brown eyes.

Heath looked around sheepishly, seeming unsure about whether Brett was serious. He pulled down on the bottom of his orange T-shirt, smoothing out some of the wrinkles. Finally he made eye contact. "I'm so sorry, and I know it was totally wrong and all, but . . ." Heath ran a nervous hand through his messy hair. Apologizing was probably not something he was used to. "But the thing is, it didn't seem like things were working out between you two anyway. And I know that's no excuse, but honestly . . ." A dreamy look came over Heath's face, and the room was silent. "I haven't felt this giddy about a girl since the days of Juliet van Pelt." Across the table, Brandon immediately shook his head, and Brett wondered who Heath was talking about. "I mean," he tried again. He looked at Brett pleadingly, the look on his face reminding her of the way Bree used to plead with their parents when she was in high school and wanted her curfew extended. "Don't you know what it feels like to like someone so much that nothing else matters?"

The Usual Suspects sat in shocked silence—Heath Ferro, sounding like a character from a chick flick? But Brett was the most shocked of all. She *did* know what it felt like to care about someone that much. But she didn't feel that way about Kara— she felt that way about *Jeremiah*. She was still in love with him, no matter how hard she'd tried to distract herself or convince herself otherwise.

But it didn't matter anymore, and Jeremiah wasn't going to hear it. First, she was a lying, cheating, teacher-sleeping-with slut. Then she was the jealous girlfriend who dumped him *again* for having tried to move on. And now she was a lesbian pyro? There was no way Jeremiah would ever love her, or even speak to her, again.

**A WAVERLY OWL KNOWS THAT WHERE THERE'S
SMOKE, THERE'S FIRE.**

"Motive," Tinsley interjected, and everyone came to attention again. "*That's* what we're looking for. Motive and opportunity."

Callie was relieved when Tinsley broke the stunned silence. Brett slumped back into Marymount's chair, and Callie tried to give her a sympathetic smile, but her gaze was trained on Dean Marymount's enormous leather-framed desk calendar.

"I think everyone in the room had an opportunity." Heath laughed, looking relieved that they weren't talking about him and Kara anymore. "Isn't that why we're all here?"

Tinsley shot Heath a look of death, her violet eyes piercing. "Okay, motive, then. We need to concentrate on motive."

Callie knew where Tinsley was headed. She glanced at Easy, who was doodling on a blank sheet of paper. After hanging out with Tinsley and Chloe for a little while at the party last night, she had found her way to Easy, hoping they'd sneak off to the woods for some alone time. But he'd mumbled some excuse about being tired and then gone home early. He did seem pretty exhausted today, so she hoped he really was just tired. But her stomach tingled nervously at the possibility that he was still suspicious of her. She'd have to be really careful today.

"I don't fucking get this at all." Benny crossed her arms in front of her, flattening her already pretty flat chest. "Couldn't the fire have just been an accident?" People started to nod in agreement.

"Whatever. Marymount wants blood," Tinsley declared, sweeping a lock of glossy hair off her shoulder. "After all the info he got from his *niece*"—she nodded her head in the direction of the silver-framed family picture, which was now sitting in the middle of the conference table—"he clearly believes someone started the fire on purpose. He just can't figure out who had the strongest motive, which is why we're all locked in here."

Tinsley's words drifted around the room, and Callie watched her smug face as she waited for someone to contradict her.

"What kind of motive?" Callie asked tentatively, toying with a strand of wavy blond hair. She glanced up at Easy, who wrinkled his forehead furiously as if to ask, *What the hell are you doing?*

"Well, let's see." Tinsley tilted her head toward the ceiling, pretending to be deep in thought. "What are some good motives? How about jealousy?"

Callie tried not to look at Jenny, who was seated directly across from her and Tinsley. She picked at one of her raggedy cuticles instead. She'd started biting her nails again recently, a bad habit she'd thought she'd given up years ago. Maybe this weekend she'd take the train to Manhattan and get a decent manicure. She could really use a spa day after all this stress.

"Jealous about what?" Brandon asked. He took a delicate swig from his bottle of Evian. Callie stared at the bottle enviously.

"That's the question," Tinsley said. Callie stole a glance at Jenny, who shifted in her seat. She was nibbling on the rim of her now-empty paper coffee cup. "Someone was jealous of something."

"Or someone," Callie added. She shrugged her shoulders casually, as if the thought had just occurred to her, and pulled her white cardigan tighter across her chest.

"Wait, are we talking about someone trying to *murder* someone else?" Sage Francis asked, her thin blond eyebrows rising skeptically. *Shut up, Sage,* Callie wanted to shout. "That's crazy."

Tinsley let out a natural-sounding laugh that only Callie recognized as fake. "Not murder." She shook her head, as if amused by Sage's outlandishness. "But maybe someone was angry and jealous enough to do something so stupid and thoughtless, it could have killed someone."

"Like who?" Easy asked defiantly, his blue eyes flashing, as if daring Tinsley to name Jenny.

Callie slunk down in her chair.

"Yeah, like who?" Julian echoed Easy's question. He'd been so quiet, Callie had almost forgotten he was there.

Callie looked at Tinsley. Her violet-eyed best friend seemed to be feeding off all the doubt in the room, drawing her strength up around her as she prepared to strike. Tinsley stared at Jenny, who at first pretended not to notice but acknowledged her when everyone else at the table stared at her, too.

"What?" Jenny finally asked, her little chin sticking out in defiance. She stared right back at Tinsley, surprising everyone. "If you're going to say something, just say it."

Tinsley smirked and Callie knew that it was over—Tinsley, once set on a course of action, was as impossible to stop as a wildfire spreading through dry brush. Ever since she'd arrived back on campus and found Jenny in her old bed, Tinsley had had it in for Jenny. Tinsley was used to being the most-talked-about person at Waverly, but Jenny, with her cute demeanor and gigantic chest, had stolen her thunder. Callie understood why Tinsley resented Jenny, though she still didn't entirely understand why she *hated* her. It wasn't like Jenny had stolen *her* boyfriend. "Well, Jenny, now that you ask . . ." Tinsley began poisonously.

"What makes *you* so innocent, Tinsley?" Julian cut her off before she could finish. Callie looked over at him, unable to believe that a freshman, no matter how cute or how tall he was, had the courage to challenge Tinsley Carmichael. The red leaves of the birch trees outside the window whipped angrily in the wind behind him, but he looked perfectly collected, as if he had an ace in his pocket and was waiting for the perfect moment to throw it down on the table. The Usual Suspects looked at Julian and then again at Tinsley, as if watching a tennis match.

Tinsley turned to face Julian. Her stomach turned over as she met his gaze. His normally warm brown eyes were narrowed. She dug her nails into her palms under the table. Did Julian really *hate* her? True, she hadn't exactly been sugaring him up recently. But if she had to be honest with herself, she'd sort of hoped that once Jenny was out of the picture, he'd come crawling back for forgiveness. But if Julian was through with her, then he might as well be as miserable as she was.

"Of course, you assume I'm the bad guy here. You're so quick to defend Jenny's innocence," she said evenly. She turned to face Jenny across the table. Jenny stared back rebelliously and refused to avert her eyes. "Jenny, why don't you tell everyone about the picture you drew in Mrs. Silver's class on Tuesday?"

Callie bit her lip, holding her breath. She couldn't look at Easy, whose eyes she felt trained on her. All the color drained from Jenny's face. Her mouth opened and closed a little, like a dying goldfish's, as she clearly scrambled to figure out how Tinsley knew about her drawing of the fire. They'd really gotten lucky. Their plan had been for Chloe to convince the dean of Jenny's guilt. But since Marymount had decided to let the *students* decide who was guilty, it was a good thing Jenny had been stupid enough to do something so incriminating—and that Chloe had been there to see it. She'd reported back to them about the drawing at the party last night. Even though Callie felt a teensy bit bad for Jenny, why would she draw something like that if she weren't, like, subconsciously trying to admit to starting the fire?

Jenny's face had turned a sickly gray, reminding Callie of

the time they'd had to dissect a frog in biology class sophomore year. Brett's face had turned exactly that color before she booted all over the lab table.

"Jeez, it was just a *drawing*," Alison spoke up suddenly, sitting forward in her chair. She looked a little nervous about challenging Tinsley, but she glanced back at Jenny, whose color had returned to a more normal-looking pink.

"What . . . uh . . . was it a drawing of?" Benny Cunningham glanced from Tinsley to Jenny, as if uncertain with whom she should ally herself, before setting her brown-eyed gaze on Tinsley.

Tinsley crossed her arms, looking as though she'd been waiting for someone to ask her that very question. "Oh, just a detailed sketch of the barn burning down. With two people in it kissing," she said casually, letting the words hang in the air.

Callie gasped. She hoped that she looked and sounded appropriately shocked. She'd never been much of an actress, but this was quite possibly the most important performance of her life.

"Who were the two people?" Easy asked, clearly annoyed. Callie stared mutely at a long scratch in the conference table. It looked as if someone had been so desperate to get out of the room that they'd tried to claw their way out.

"You asked the question," Tinsley drawled, putting her palms on the table and rising to her feet, her emerald green dress draping regally around her slim, perfect figure. She leaned forward intimidatingly, looking so much like a little lawyer that even Easy's father would have been impressed. "And now Jenny's going to tell you the answer."

Callie felt Easy's smoldering anger burn through her clothes. Her tongue felt heavy, as if it were a cold, wet sponge stuck in her mouth, and she suddenly felt like *she* might be the one to vomit all over the table. Just knowing that Easy was angry made her wonder if the whole thing was worth it, but she'd gone too far to back out now.

"How do you even know about the drawing?" Jenny demanded, finally finding her voice. "Have you been *spying* on me?" She sharpened her tongue with as much anger as she could muster, but she was still a little bit afraid of Tinsley. Did everyone think that just because she'd drawn a picture of the burning barn, she'd actually burned it down? That was totally crazy. But then, so was this whole situation.

"Are you denying it?" Tinsley paced by the window like a prosecutor on TV. Jenny had the sense that she'd been waiting for this moment—maybe since the second her vintage Fendi boots had set foot back on campus and she'd found Jenny in her room. Tinsley had hated Jenny long before anything had even happened between her and Julian, although that must have been the final straw.

"But how—" Jenny cut herself off rather than repeat her question. She felt the room starting to spin, like something in *Willy Wonka and the Chocolate Factory*. Except instead of Johnny Depp, it was Tinsley Carmichael pulling the strings. She couldn't think of anything to say that wouldn't make her sound guilty, and even Alison and Brett and Brandon and

Julian, people she'd thought would be on her side, were wait-ing expectantly for her to say something in her own defense.

"It doesn't matter how I know," Tinsley snapped. "Just answer the question."

Jenny could sense the restlessness in the room. Even Julian was looking at her with a curious expression in his big brown eyes. "It's not a big deal," she tried to explain, focusing on Brett, who had to know she was innocent. "Mrs. Silver, you know how she is." Jenny brushed her curly hair away from her face, feeling the heat in the room and wishing she had a glass of water. She stared at Brandon's bottle of Evian longingly, already feeling herself losing her train of thought. "She had us do this drawing, you know, with our eyes closed," Jenny explained, her breathing becoming labored as she fumbled through the words. "And I was having a hard time with it. I guess I was stressed out by . . . well, we're all stressed out, right? This whole thing has us stressed out, right?"

Jenny looked around the room for affirmation, but the Usual Suspects—her supposed friends—averted their eyes.

"So . . ." Tinsley prompted, resting against the window ledge, her arms still crossed over her chest. "Your drawing?" she asked coldly.

"It was a picture of the fire," Jenny answered, feeling miser-able, cursing Mrs. Silver for pushing her so hard to get into her subconscious. Why couldn't she have just drawn some stupid random rectangles, like Alison?

"Big deal." Heath spoke up. He glanced at Jenny, and she thought of her first night at Waverly, when she'd made out with him. "No offense. I'm sure it's a Picasso or a Rembrandt or whatever." She'd been so eager to fit in then, so excited about her brand-new life at boarding school. Now two boys had lied to her and broken her heart, and the popular girls clearly wanted her dead. Was her life any better than it had been before? No, it was a thousand times worse.

Tinsley shot Heath a glare that silenced him. Of course he was in her power, too. "What else was in the picture?" she asked.

"What do you mean?" Jenny asked innocently. She was hoping Julian or Heath would jump in again, or Brett, and derail Tinsley's cross-examination. But no one said anything, and she stared at the silly red watch on her wrist. She wished she were anywhere but here—on the sweaty, crowded 2 train in the Bronx after a Yankees loss, even. Anywhere.

"Did you draw two people in the fire?" Tinsley asked point-blank. Before Jenny could open her mouth—she wasn't sure what she was going to say; if only she were capable of the kind of first-class lying she'd witnessed in her short time at Waverly—Tinsley added, "And wasn't it Callie and Easy you drew in the burning barn?"

Someone in the corner gasped. Jenny hoped it wasn't Julian.

"Is that true?" Benny clapped a delicate hand to her mouth. "That's so . . ." Her words trailed off.

"Weren't you so jealous of Callie and Easy that you decided to burn the barn down when you saw them go inside?" Tinsley put her hands on her hips, drumming her fingers on her slim waistline.

"That's enough. Knock it off." Easy sat up in his chair, a chagrined look on his face. "It was just a drawing. Stop being such a pushy bitch."

Jenny felt a surge of gratitude, but before she could say anything else, the door flew open, and in one smooth motion, Dean Marymount breezed in and stood in the center of the room.

"So," he said, hands in the pockets of his blazer. Jenny felt like she was about to pass out. What kind of lazy dean was he? Instead of interviewing students, gathering evidence, and talking to the police like he should have, he'd let the bullies have their way. "Have you come to a decision?"

Jenny glanced around. Everyone was staring back at her. Even Julian was looking at her like he didn't recognize her. She gripped the table, conscious only of one thing: She'd never really belonged at Waverly to begin with. It was obvious that if everyone was so quick to turn on her, none of them really cared about her. At the start of the semester, all she'd wanted was to make friends and feel like she belonged. But was anyone present ever really her friend? She'd thought Callie was briefly, but she'd been so very wrong about that. Brett certainly cared about her, but she'd been too caught up recently with whatever was happening with Kara to even ask how Jenny was doing. Her entire relationship with Easy now felt like a mirage. And Julian's kisses were completely tainted by the fact that he'd lied to her, too.

"Well?" Marymount demanded, a note of impatience in his voice. No one spoke.

Jenny looked around. One of them was guilty, but suddenly,

it didn't really matter who. She just knew she had to get out of that suffocating room.

"*I did it*, all right?" She pushed her heavy chair back from the table with a screech, her fingertips burning against the wood. She could feel her cheeks flush, and before anyone could stop her, she marched straight out of the room.

Hot tears blinded Jenny as she tore down the steps and sprinted across the quad to Dumbarton. It was over—boarding school, boys, hanging out with the in crowd. She was going to her room to pack her bags and leave, forever.

OwlNet   Email Inbox

From: DeanMarymount@waverly.edu
To: Waverly Student Body
Date: Wednesday, October 16, 12:34 P.M.
Subject: Justice

My fellow Owls,

The matter of the fire at the Miller farm has been resolved. A student has come forward and confessed to the crime. She will be removed from campus immediately.

I am counting on you to take this as a serious warning. In the future, you will behave like proper Waverly Owls.

Gratefully,

Dean Marymount

KaraWhalen: I just woke up. WTF happened?

HeathFerro: Some shit went down. Short answer: Jenny confessed.

KaraWhalen: What??? No way!

HeathFerro: Sux, I kno. But maybe U should talk to Brett.

KaraWhalen: Y?

HeathFerro: Just talk to her.

KaraWhalen: OK . . .

HeathFerro: Actually, if you come over I'll tell you everything. ;)

A WAVERLY OWL KNOWS THE DIFFERENCE
BETWEEN GOODBYE AND FAREWELL.

Jenny folded her last pair of Banana Republic jeans into her dad's old brown Samsonite. The faded HUGS NOT BOMBS sticker near the handle caught her eye, and she instantly wondered how the hell she was going to explain this to her dad. She hadn't even responded to his e-mail that was written in the voice of their cat. Whatever. She had a whole train ride into the city to figure it out. She'd packed her enormous red-and-white polka-dotted LeSportsac with lightning speed, throwing her books and clothes and makeup haphazardly inside, not caring if she was leaving anything behind. It hadn't seemed that long ago that she'd gotten out of the cab and trudged up the Waverly driveway, hauling everything she owned.

Now she looked back on that Jenny—the Old Jenny who wanted to be New Jenny—with disdain. She couldn't believe she'd been so naive as to think that her entire life was going to change for the better when she went to boarding school. Back in the city, she'd always managed to get herself into trouble—she'd even wound up on Page Six—but here, she thought she'd be a cooler, more composed version of herself. But she hadn't even lasted two months. It was a small blip in her life. Someday she'd be a creaky old lady in a creaky old rocker with boobs down to her knees, and she might not even remember she ever went to boarding school.

Jenny felt tears welling in her eyes, and her throat tightening. How could she forget Easy sketching her, or Julian's kiss at the farm, or manicure nights with Brett? But right now, those things were completely overshadowed by the dark cloud that was Tinsley Carmichael. Jenny still couldn't believe what Tinsley had done, but even more unbelievable was the idea that Tinsley hated her enough to do it. It felt terrible to be that hated.

Jenny sat down on the top of the overstuffed Samsonite, trying to get the latches to click. She didn't know where the confession had come from, but a sense of relief had washed over her as she stormed out of Dean Marymount's office. She was *free*. No more worrying about who was saying what about her, or what dark forces were conspiring against her.

She whirled around at the sound of tapping on her door, wondering if Tinsley or Callie had come to laugh at her as she packed her things. Instead, Easy was leaning in the doorway, his hands in the pockets of his faded green cargos, his dark curls falling over his forehead.

"You really going?" he asked softly. His eyes wandered

across the room, landing on her empty bed, the soft sheets already stuffed into her duffel, along with the scratchy baby blue blanket her dad had sent to school with her.

"I'm expelled," Jenny said flatly. "That's that."

Easy scratched the back of his neck. She felt his eyes on her face, but she turned away to concentrate on the suitcase latches, willing them to close. "Yeah, but—" He didn't finish his sentence and Jenny stood still, waiting. "But you didn't really have anything to do with the fire, right?"

Jenny didn't answer. She didn't trust her voice right now. She turned back to her suitcase so her face wouldn't betray her emotions. It had been sweet of Easy to try and defend her against Tinsley—she appreciated it, really. But it was too little, too late.

"Hey," Easy said. She was about to turn around, thinking he wanted her to face him, but she heard Brett's voice say "hey" back. The Samsonite latch finally clicked into place, and Jenny grabbed the L.L. Bean tote her dad had sent her. He'd had it monogrammed with the letters *JAH* even though her middle name was Tallulah. He'd told her the reggae-loving stoners would get the joke, even if Jenny didn't. She stuffed her colorful sock balls inside, thankful that she'd already packed all her underwear and oversize granny bras before any visitors arrived.

"Well, Marymount's happier than shit." Brett exhaled, her voice sounding lighter than her worried, pale face looked. "It's like he solved the Kennedy assassination or something."

Jenny pursed her lips. "Good," was all she said.

Alison suddenly appeared behind Brett. "Ugh," she cried

out when she saw Jenny packing. "Are you *serious?*" she asked, pushing her way through. "You can't be serious."

Jenny shrugged and stared helplessly at Alison's concerned, almond-shaped eyes. It was all she could do to dam up the tears she wanted to spill all over her half-empty dorm room. The truth was, as much as she was trying to convince herself otherwise, she loved these people, and she loved boarding school.

The room grew smaller as Brandon wedged his way through the doorway, the light, airy scent of his Acqua di Gio cologne filling the air. "Don't leave," he said to Jenny, his voice soft and sweet, making Jenny kind of wish she'd kissed him once, just to see what it was like. But then, he hadn't exactly stood up for her at the meeting, either. "We all know you didn't do it."

"But whoever did totally sucks," Brett said, going up to Jenny and putting her arm around her. She was a good five inches taller than Jenny, and Jenny's head fit comfortably into the crook of her arm. "I can't believe someone is going to get away with arson and you're leaving. It's just not fair."

"We can go to Marymount and say that you didn't have anything to do with it," Alison said shakily, probably feeling guilty about the whole art-class thing, although it hadn't been her fault. Jenny had the feeling that she'd be where she was right now even if she hadn't drawn that picture of Easy and Callie in the fire.

"Yes!" Brett agreed, dropping her arm to turn toward Alison. "I'll go with you."

"No, don't." Jenny was surprised at the authority in her voice. She pulled her suitcase off her bed and let it hit the bare wood floor with a loud, ominous thud. "It doesn't matter. He wouldn't believe you anyway." She swallowed the lump in her throat. "Maybe it's for the best."

"It's like we have a murderer wandering free among us." Brett shook her wild, fire engine red hair. Jenny looked at her friend and thought about how much she was going to miss her. They'd still e-mail, right?

No one said anything, and a dark silence enveloped the room.

"Excuse me," a voice said. Jenny recognized Julian's voice and her heart skipped. Everyone turned to him expectantly, as if he were the governor calling with a last-minute stay of execution. "Could I . . . uh . . . just talk to Jenny, for a minute? Alone?" Jenny stuffed a couple of J.Crew sweaters from her last drawer into her tote, trying not to think how nice it sounded to hear her name on Julian's lips. Easy backed out of the doorway, nodding at Jenny as he disappeared down the hall. Brett and Brandon and Alison shuffled out, too. Julian leaned against the door to close it. His head almost reached the top of the doorway. "How are you doing?"

Jenny shrugged. She didn't know the answer to that question. Instead, she grabbed another sweater—the thick, oatmeal-colored hoodie her father had sent her along with the JAH tote bag—and shoved it, unceremoniously, into her bag.

"That was some pretty rough stuff in there," Julian said, and immediately, the image of Tinsley staring her down came back to mind. "But why . . . why did you take the blame? You didn't do it—you were with me."

"I don't want to talk about it," Jenny said, not really meaning it, but she knew talk wasn't going to change anything that happened. She'd confessed, and Marymount had expelled her. It was over. She was going home. The zipper quivered as she tugged it closed.

"I just can't, you know . . ." A quiver worked its way into Julian's usually calm voice, and his brown eyes looked like a sad puppy's. "Don't go like this. It's not right."

"Life is full of things that aren't right," Jenny said, surprised by how matter-of-fact her voice sounded.

"I know you," Julian said, regaining his composure a little. He rested his elbow on the top of Jenny's now-empty dresser. He was too tall for her, anyway, Jenny realized wistfully. "Why are you pretending you're not devastated?"

"I'm not the one pretending," Jenny shot back. She heaved her duffel off the floor and tossed it next to her suitcase. The amount of venom flowing through her scared her a little.

"I never pretended anything." Julian stared down at the toes of his gray canvas Vans. "Okay, maybe I did pretend the whole thing with Tinsley never happened." He paused. "But only because I really, really wished it hadn't."

Jenny sat down on what was left of her bed. She felt as sad and empty as the bare mattress looked. "It doesn't work that way."

Julian bit his lip. In his faded blue polo and beat-up khakis, he looked like one of the St. Jude's boys she used to see playing Frisbee in Central Park. Jenny wondered what would have happened if she'd met him like that—away from Waverly, and away from Tinsley Carmichael. Would they have stood a chance? "That morning after the fire when we were walking in the woods, I wanted to tell you about Tinsley," he said, pulling open an empty dresser drawer and closing it again.

"So, why didn't you?" she demanded, pulling her knees up to her chest and wrapping her arms around them. "Why didn't you tell me about it before we even kissed?"

Julian couldn't look at her. His head was hanging, and he picked up a stray bobby pin from the top of her dresser and twirled it between his fingers. "Because everything with you just . . . felt so good. I didn't want to fuck it up."

Jenny felt herself starting to melt. *Julian*. But even if she forgave him, what was the point? She was leaving, on the next train out of Rhinecliff.

"And I didn't tell you later, because . . . because I wanted to protect you from Tinsley." His brown eyes were bloodshot and sad. A shiver ran down her spine, and she zipped up her H&M knock-off Stella McCartney army green jacket. "I'm pretty sure *she* started the fire, but I was afraid if she found out about us, she'd try to pin it on you."

"Why would she do that?" Jenny asked, trying to keep her voice even. The question wasn't really meant for Julian; it was the question she kept trying to answer herself. She kicked at her suitcase, not caring if she scraped up the hardwood floors.

"Because I like you more than I liked her. I like you a whole lot."

Jenny hoped those words would be her lasting memory, long after the bitterness had drained from her body. *I like you a whole lot.* That was a nice going-away present. She could sense Julian's desire for closure—for whatever, forgiveness—but she couldn't give it to him. The problem was, she wasn't even that mad at him—she was just furious with herself for being so incredibly stupid. Time and time again.

"Don't worry about it." She hiked her LeSportsac over her shoulder and grabbed her purple suede school bag stuffed with the books she wanted to keep, leaving the rest on her bookshelves for Callie, or whoever moved back in, to deal with. "At least we had some fun, right?" Her voice sounded breezy and false, even to her. She couldn't look at him again, and instead focused on picking up her overloaded suitcase with her empty hand. In her closet, her maroon Waverly blazer looked tiny and alone.

"Can I . . . help you?" Julian asked awkwardly, standing up to his full height.

"No." Jenny picked up the L.L. Bean tote and grabbed the handle of her Samsonite. She pushed through the doorway, her bags almost getting stuck, before turning around. Julian stood in the middle of the room, looking lost. Every ounce of her wanted to drop her bags and throw her arms around his shoulders and kiss him. But she couldn't.

She walked away, feeling resolved. Maybe it wasn't all for nothing. Maybe she'd learned something from each false friendship and each failed hookup. Maybe at her next school, she *would* be the cool and composed person she'd always wanted to be.

Maybe.

From: TinsleyCarmichael@waverly.edu
To: chloe.marymount@gmail.com
Date: Wednesday, October 16, 12:41 P.M.
Subject: RE: RE: How's it going?

Hey kid,

Hope you enjoyed your stay at Waverly. Thanks for all your help. You did the right thing.

Tinsley

From: chloe.marymount@gmail.com
To: TinsleyCarmichael@waverly.edu
Date: Wednesday, October 16, 12:50 P.M.
Subject: RE: RE: RE: How's it going?

Hi Tinsley!

Thanks for showing me such a good time at the party last night . . . the train ride home this morning wasn't so fun though. ;) But I'm so glad things happened with Sam. I think he really likes me!

Anyway, can't wait to hang with you at Waverly next year.

XOXO

Chloe

TinsleyCarmichael: Hey, Julian. Too bad you'll have to say goodbye to your artsy little girlfriend—she was really, um, talented.

TinsleyCarmichael: If you're too heartbroken to reply, I understand.

KaraWhalen: I heard about what happened. It's so awful.

BrettMesserschmidt: Yeah, poor Jenny. But where were you?

KaraWhalen: Passed out. Can't believe I missed the meeting.

BrettMesserschmidt: Well, it's prob. better you weren't there. Guess you had fun last night huh?

KaraWhalen: About that . . . I am so sorry. Can we talk about it?

BrettMesserschmidt: Honestly, there's not much to say.

KaraWhalen: Oh.

BrettMesserschmidt: I mean that in a good way.

KaraWhalen: Oh!

BrettMesserschmidt: Friends?

KaraWhalen: Absolutely.

BrettMesserschmidt: So does this mean I'm going to be spending a lot of time with Heath? ;)

KaraWhalen: We'll see. . . .

26

A WAVERLY OWL KNOWS THAT TEXT MESSAGES
ARE PRIVATE.

Easy stood outside Dumbarton, kicking his toe against the hard stone step. He looked up to see Callie headed toward him up the walk, the flouncy skirt of her blue-and-white dress swirling around her knees in the wind, smiling as if nothing out of the ordinary had happened.

"What's going on?" Callie asked, teetering a little on her skinny navy heels. She tilted her head in concern, as if she had no idea what could possibly be wrong.

Easy just stared at her. He'd always known Callie would make a wonderful actress—she was excellent at coming up with her own versions of the truth and sticking to them. "I just came from Jenny's."

Callie tensed up, gripping the strap of her distressed black bag with the oversize silver buckles. "Why?"

"What do you mean, 'Why'? I wanted to say goodbye."

"Oh." A look of relief washed over her pale face.

"Aren't you going to go see her before she leaves?" he asked. He recognized his father's demanding voice in his own, but so what? He was angry, and there was no use pretending he wasn't.

Callie shrugged, staring down at her hands as if trying to decide whether she needed a manicure or not.

"Didn't she used to be your friend?" Easy asked, kicking at the edge of the step with frustration. The sun had come out, and he had to squint to see her.

"She *used* to be," Callie spat back, suddenly animated. Her hazel eyes flashed with anger that must have been lurking right beneath the surface. "Before she started spreading rumors about us."

"But you didn't start any rumors about *her,* right?" Easy ran a hand through his messy curls. He had wanted that question to come out a little softer than it did, but it was too late.

"What are you talking about?" Callie crossed her arms over her flat chest.

"How did Tinsley know about Jenny's drawing?" Easy was afraid to hear the answer. If Tinsley and Callie were getting people to spy on Jenny, that was beyond low. Especially somewhere like art class, which Easy had always thought of as a sanctuary, a place safe from all the gossiping and backstabbing that went on at Waverly.

"Why?" Callie's voice shook, and she bit her pink, glossy lip like she was on the verge of tears. All for show, Easy thought, bitterly. "Are you still in love with her?"

"*What?*" Easy shoved his hands in the pockets of his cargos to hide the fists of fury that had involuntarily formed. He couldn't even think about answering that—not after he and Callie had spent the last five days together every chance they had. She knew better than to ask a question like that. "Just answer me this: Did you get someone to spy on Jenny?"

Callie was dying to pull her Oliver Peoples sunglasses from her bag and throw them on her face, just to put some sort of barrier up against Easy's demanding stare. But she didn't want to look guilty—especially since he already seemed to think she was. "Why are you yelling at me?" she asked softly, letting all the anger—at him defending Jenny *yet again*—drain from her voice. "Jenny admitted that she started the fire. What's done is done."

"You really think she did it?" Easy asked plainly.

Callie demurred, staring at the toes of her navy Isabella Fiore pumps. "She *said* she did."

"How do you know it wasn't us, smoking in the barn?" Easy's voice rose as he asked the question, and lost its sweet southern tinge. "Jenny's getting expelled is no joke. Do you realize how serious this is?" He was squinting in the sun, but it felt like he was glaring at her.

Callie *did* realize how serious it was. But what choice did she have? She hadn't wanted either one of them to go home. Jenny was just too easy a target. And it had been Tinsley's plan, anyway, not Callie's. Even if she'd refused to go along with it, Tinsley would have carried the plan out without her, and everything would have happened exactly as it had. "It was all Tinsley," Callie blurted out before realizing what she was saying.

Easy sat down on the step and arched his back against the hard stone column. He took his hands out of his pockets, much to her relief. She'd been able to see his fists through his cargos and was a little afraid of him. Not that he'd, like, hit her or anything—but she'd never seen him so mad. "You didn't have *anything* to do with it?" he asked skeptically, raising a dark eyebrow.

"It was Tinsley's plan," Callie lied, fiddling with one of the pearl buttons on her cardigan. "She had it in for Jenny from day one, when she found her in her bed. She got that Chloe girl, the prospective, to spy on her. Honest." Callie looked him in his deep blue eyes and crossed her heart like she had in grade school when she was lying through her teeth. "I didn't know about it until it was already done."

Easy seemed to relax a little, and Callie took the opportunity to sit down on the steps next to him. She took his calloused hand in hers. He squeezed hers back, and she could feel her shoulders slump as her body relaxed. "Are we okay?" she asked softly, leaning in to nuzzle against him.

"Yeah," Easy whispered back, gently cradling her in the crook of his broad shoulder. His neck was soft and warm and inviting, and she felt like she was back where she belonged. He kissed her head, and Callie let go of all the tension in her body, collapsing into his arms in relief.

But as Callie shifted on the stone step, her skinny silver Razr tumbled out of her Fendi bag, landing with a crack on the first step, out of her reach. It immediately buzzed to life, vibrating its way onto the grass. Before she could do anything to stop him, Easy stood and picked up the phone for her, reaching out to hand it back to her. But he stopped when he saw who the text was from. "Speak of the devil," he said. He pressed a button and his handsome face turned ghostly pale.

"Give it back!" Callie reached for the phone, feeling like she was about to be sick.

Easy's brow furrowed as he read the message. *"Congrats to us on a job well done."* His voice was hard and full of mocking. *"It worked. The bitch is gone. Let's drink to that,"* he read off the little screen.

"It's not what you think." Callie got to her feet, her heels wobbling beneath her. "You know how Tinsley is—she's just making noise."

Easy didn't seem to have heard a word she said. "Nice." He handed her the phone, shaking his head as if to shake all the lies from his ears.

"Easy!" Callie's eyes stung with hot tears. "You can't just leave me like this."

But apparently he could.

From: JenniferHumphrey@waverly.edu
To: RufusHumphrey@poetsonline.com
Date: Wednesday, October 16, 2:49 P.M.
Subject: RE: Meow!

Dear Marx the Cat—

Looks like you've gotten your wish, I'm going to be home later tonight. I'll explain everything once I get there. Tell Vanessa she can stay in my room, I'll stay on the couch for now.

Love you guys, see you soon.

Jenny

A WAVERLY OWL HOLDS HER HEAD UP HIGH—EVEN
WHEN SHE'S NO LONGER A WAVERLY OWL.

Jenny hoisted her beat-up duffel onto her shoulder and walked toward the waiting yellow taxi. Just a short cab ride and a few hours on the train separated her from home, from her ramshackle but inviting apartment on the Upper West Side; her old room; her crazy, wonderful, gastronomically challenged father; and her beloved cat. Footsteps echoed behind her and her heart skipped a beat. She hoped it was Julian, or maybe Easy . . . but when she spun around, she saw Dean Marymount instead, his Waverly tie flying over his shoulder as he sprinted toward her. A faint cold fear crept up Jenny's spine. What other punishment did Marymount want to inflict before she got in the cab and disappeared forever? Was he going to handcuff her or something?

Jenny took one last look at the campus behind him. She really did love Waverly, with its stately redbrick buildings, its rosy-faced students, its tradition. She loved living in a dorm, playing field hockey, going to parties in the woods. Kissing boys and hanging out with all her new friends. She was really going to miss it.

"Wait!" Marymount called out, an annoyed look on his face. He slowed to a jog and then stopped, resting his hands on his khaki-clad knees. His graying sandy hair was spread in strings across his growing bald spot.

Should she just tell him to get a toupee and make a break for it?

"Mrs. Miller just called," he tried to explain, still breathing heavily. He straightened up and adjusted his tie.

Jenny screwed up her face, wondering what this was all about. Did the old lady want the chance to personally reprimand the arsonist? Would she be forced to clean up the wreckage, one charred piece of wood at a time? Would she be sent to jail? She hadn't thought of that. Wasn't she too young?

"She insists the whole thing was . . . an accident." Marymount went on, pulling down on his sweater and collecting himself. "She claims one of her *cows* started the fire." His cold blue eyes scanned Jenny carefully, as if waiting to pounce on the first betrayed emotion. But she was too stunned to move a muscle. "I don't see how a cow could start a fire. However"—he squinted into the sun—"she says she's sure it was one of her cows. What do you think about that?" He put his hands on his hips, waiting for her answer.

Jenny had a hard time processing what exactly it was Marymount was saying. She set her bag down on the gravelly driveway, rubbing her numbed shoulder. Did he really want her to answer that question? Cows starting fires? She didn't even know what the hell he was talking about. But wait, was he trying to say she wasn't expelled after all?

"Anyway, she said she didn't want anyone at Waverly to be blamed," Marymount continued, his voice full of suspicion. "Personally, I think she's a crazy old woman who has lived alone for too long, but . . ." He scratched his head, and some of the carefully placed strings of hair shifted, revealing his shiny bald head.

The cabdriver honked his horn impatiently and Marymount glanced toward the waiting car.

"If a Waverly student did start the fire, they'd have to be expelled," Marymount said, his eyes settling again on Jenny's round face. "No way around it. Do you agree?"

"But it was the cows," Jenny answered slowly, starting to get the impression that while Marymount didn't believe Mrs. Miller's story, he wasn't convinced Jenny was guilty, either. "Right?"

Marymount nodded slowly, rubbing his sweaty forehead with his left hand, his gold wedding band glinting in the bright sun. "Yes, right." He rolled his eyes. "So . . . it looks like I'm going to have to decline your, ahem, *confession*."

Jenny looked back toward campus, at the perfect green lawns and perfectly lush trees, at the perfect piles of leaves. Behind her, the cabdriver revved his engine. It took her a second to convince herself that Marymount wasn't kidding, that it wasn't some cruel joke. Her heart began to race.

"You'd better get to class, Ms. Humphrey." Marymount stared her down, tapping a finger against the silver watch on his wrist.

Jenny just stared back at him, pressing her lips together. She couldn't wait to see the look on everyone's face when they saw her back in Dumbarton, back in her old room. Back in her classes. She'd be back in the dining hall for dinner. Tonight was her favorite—make-your-own-pita-pizza night. And tomorrow, Jenny would stride across Waverly's green campus and a hundred Owls would whisper her name.

She was *back*.

HeathFerro: Old lady Miller saves the day! Someone buy that bat a beer!

JulianMcCafferty: What are you talking about, Ferro?

HeathFerro: U didn't hear? She told Marymount her COWS set the fire—no expulsions necessary.

JulianMcCafferty: Wait, so Jenny's staying?

HeathFerro: Why, were U already planning your reunion w/ Tinsley?

OwlNet

Instant Message Inbox

SageFrancis: OMG, Celine was at the bank just now and old lady Miller was depositing a FAT check. Told the clerk she's going to build a guesthouse where the barn was.

BrandonBuchanan: Huh. Insurance kicked in?

SageFrancis: Insurance doesn't cut checks that quickly.

BrandonBuchanan: You think someone bribed her to save Jenny?

SageFrancis: Exactly, Sherlock. Who do you think it was? My guess is someone rich and male. . . .

BrandonBuchanan: I'd like to thank him. Jenny's too sweet to get expelled.

SageFrancis: Watch out, you're making me jealous.

BrandonBuchanan: That's the idea.

TinsleyCarmichael: Fucking cows?!

CallieVernon: Whatever. That's the least of my problems.

TinsleyCarmichael: Y?

CallieVernon: EZ found out what we did. I think it's over.

TinsleyCarmichael: Shit. I'm sorry.

CallieVernon: You should be.

TinsleyCarmichael: What's that mean?

CallieVernon: It means I'm too upset to talk to you right now.

BrettMesserschmidt: Is it for real? Are you back?

JennyHumphrey: I guess so! So weird. An hour ago, I was expelled. Now I'm back.

BrettMesserschmidt: Well, I'M thrilled . . . and so are a ton of other people.

JennyHumphrey: I can think of a few who aren't.

BrettMesserschmidt: Fuck 'em. You heard about Mrs. Miller, right? She was totally bribed by someone to say the cows did it.

JennyHumphrey: What R U talking about? Bribed?

BrettMesserschmidt: Someone REALLY didn't want you to go. Enough to PAY for you to stay.

JennyHumphrey: That's crazy. . . .

BrettMesserschmidt: Welcome back, babe. Now it's time to figure out who your secret admirer is! And don't worry, Inspector M is on the case.

JennyHumphrey: Oooh, I've always wanted a secret admirer. . . .

Turn the page for a sneak peak of

gossip girl
the carlyles

Created by the #1 *New York Times* bestselling author
Cecily von Ziegesar

hey people!

Surprised to hear from me? Don't be. While the rest of us may be learning the finer points of flip cup and experiencing our first cross-campus walks of shame, you should know by now *I'd* never be that predictable. Instead of uncorking the Cristal like all of you did when you got your acceptance letters (or for some of you unfortunates, that email saying you were off the wait list), I read the fine print. There's a little "Get Out of Jail Free" card known as the deferral. So while all of you are in Connecticut and Rhode Island with roomies whose asses are busting out of their Juicys from too many trips to the dining hall fro-yo machine, I'll be here enjoying one more year on the Upper East Side.

Why, you ask? After watching some of last year's seniors shop at ABC Carpet & Home for last-minute dorm décor (not sure how well those Venetian cut glass chandeliers are going to fit above the bunk beds in your freshman doubles, kiddies), I saw three of the most fabulous human beings on the planet emerge from Blair Waldorf's old apartment, including one amazing male specimen. Sure, these new kids on the block (Manhattan's most exclusive block, that is) look like they exploded from an Abercrombie & Fitch catalog, but we don't usually get 'em that fresh in these parts. And there's nothing like fresh meat to make things really interesting.

You all probably have to go read Ovid and drink a Natty Ice in your new

8 x 10 dorm room, but don't worry, I'll be here drinking Veuve mimosas at Balthazar, reporting on what you're missing. With these three in town, I just know it's going to be another wild and wicked year. . . .

sightings

O running in Central Park, without a shirt. Does he *own* any shirts? Let's hope not! . . . **A** trying on a silver-sequined Marni minidress in the dressing room of Bergdorf's. Didn't anyone tell her Constance has a dress code? . . . And her sister **B** in FAO Schwartz, clinging to a dude in a barn-red NANTUCKET HIGH hoodie putting stuffed animals in inappropriate poses and taking pictures. Is *that* what they do for fun where they're from?

your mail

Dear GG,
So, my mom went to Constance Billard like a million years ago with the triplets' mom and she told me the reason they moved here is because **A** slept with the entire island—boys *and* girls. And then **B** is, like, this crazy brilliant genius who's mentally unstable and never washes her clothes. And **O** apparently swims up to Nantucket on the weekends in a Speedo. Is that true?
—3some

Dear 3,
Interesting. From what I've seen, **A** looks pretty innocent. But we all know looks can be deceiving. We'll see how brilliantly **B** does in the city. As for **O**, Nantucket's a long way away, so I doubt he can swim that far. But if he *can* . . . I've got one word for you: *endurance*. Exactly what I look for in a man.
—GG

Q: Dear GG,

So, I just moved here and I love New York!!!!! Do you have any advice to make this year the best year ever?

—SMLLTWNGRL

A: Dear STG,

All I can say is be careful. Manhattan is a pretty small place itself, albeit much more fabulous than wherever you came from. No matter what you do, and no matter where you are, *somebody* is watching. And it's not going to be gossiped about in your high school cafeteria—in this town, it's bound to hit Page Six. *If* you're interesting or important enough to be gossiped about, that is. One can only hope.

—GG

Q: Dear GG,

I bet you're just saying you deferred from college because you didn't get in anywhere. Also, I heard that a certain monkey-owning dude never made it to West Point and I think it's pretty mysterious that he's still here and so are you. Are you really a girl??

RUCHUCKB

A: Dear RUCHUCKB,

I'm flattered that my continued presence is spawning conspiracy theories. Sorry to disappoint, but I am as feminine as they come, without a pet monkey in sight. As for your first comment, I got in everywhere I applied. But why bother expanding your horizons (and your behind) when everyone knows Manhattan is the center of the universe?

—GG

Time for me to prep for fashion week. And for you to prep for the first day of school. Hope those of you who went off to college are going easy on the Tater Tots if you want to fit into Chloé's amazing new collection. Fashion week gets better every year.

Just like me.

You know you love me,

gossip girl

the best things in life are free

The grand store awnings and the glittering pavement of Madison Avenue welcomed Avery Carlyle, the newest resident of Manhattan's Golden Mile, with each Fendi-heeled step. Every preppy boy in a rumpled Pink dress shirt and Brooks Brothers khakis and girl loaded down with Hermès and Chanel shopping bags that she passed was like an oasis in the desert of her life. She couldn't wait until tomorrow, when she would start school at Manhattan's exclusive Constance Billard School for Girls and her life would finally begin.

Avery was born in Nantucket, Massachusetts, the smallest, sandiest, boringest island on the East Coast and the rest of the universe. Her trips to New York had always been limited to one week a year at Christmas, when all the Carlyles—mom Edie and triplets Owen, Avery, and Baby—would gather to celebrate the holidays with their grandmother, the venerable socialite and philanthropist Avery Carlyle the first. When grandmother Avery passed away in May, Avery the second was devastated—she'd always been close with her namesake, and she took the loss harder than anyone in her family. But there was a silver lining.

Isn't there always?

Her hippie artist mother, Edie, found that sorting through the late Avery's affairs was impossible from the tiny island off the coast of Cape Cod, so she moved the triplets to the city and enrolled Avery and Baby at Constance Billard and Owen at the equally expensive and exclusive St. Jude's School for Boys. Plus, it seemed more appropriate to grieve for their grandmother here. Avery was resolved to do her grandma proud. Starting with a brand-new wardrobe.

She paused at the large plate glass windows of the Calvin Klein boutique on the corner of Sixty-second Street and took in her reflection. With her long wheat-colored blond hair wrapped in a Pucci print headscarf and a peony pink Diane von Furstenburg wrap dress hugging her athletic frame, Avery looked like any Upper East Sider out for a stroll. In Nantucket, where fleece was party attire and a party was drinking a six-pack of Molson on the beach, Avery had always been out of her element. But this year it was all going to be different. Finally, she was where she belonged.

Avery tore herself away from the shopwindow and continued to walk down Madison. Her destination today was Barneys, the legendary Upper East Side department store, and her mission was to find the perfect bag for the first day of the rest of her life. She'd been momentarily disappointed when her mother, a Constance alum herself, had reminded her about the school's mandatory uniforms—but had quickly realized that accessories were key. The perfect bag would broadcast to her new class-mates everything she wanted them to know about her: that she believed in classic beauty, that she loved to have fun, that she was one of them.

Avery reached the door to Barneys and smiled as the dapper doorman held it open. She breathed in deeply as she entered, the achingly familiar scent of Creed Fleurissimo hitting her along with the AC. It had been her grandmother's favorite perfume, and Avery could practically feel her grandmother's touch steering her away from an oversize apple-green Marc Jacobs bag and toward the true designer purses.

Avery walked through the luxury handbag department, reverently touching the crocodile skin and soft leathers. Her eyes stopped on a cognac-colored Givenchy satchel and she felt her stomach flutter. Its gold buckles reminded her of the antique chest she'd left behind in Nantucket. She'd always imagined some blue-blooded royalty had dropped the trunk into the Atlantic as their ancient ship sank and that it was recovered by a bearded lobsterman years after their romantic death.

"Exquisite piece," Avery heard a smooth voice over her shoulder. She turned around and took in the saleslady behind her. She was in her mid-forties, with gray-streaked hair pulled back into a sleek bun.

"It's beautiful," Avery agreed, wishing the saleslady would disappear. She wanted this moment to be pure: a moment between her and the purse.

"Limited edition," the saleslady noted. Her name tag read Natalie. "It was actually claimed, but we never heard back from the buyer. . . . Would you be interested?" Natalie raised her perfectly plucked eyebrows.

Avery nodded, transfixed. She loved the fact that it was limited edition, that she'd be the only person at her school with this unique purse. She glanced at the price tag—$4,000. Eek. But she hadn't really bought that much so far, and wasn't that what

Edie's new accountant, Alan, was for? Besides, as Grandmother Avery had once reminded her when she'd admired a vintage Hermès Kelly bag: Handbags never die. Men do. This bag was forever.

"I'll take it," she said confidently, her just-manicured petal pink fingernails reaching toward the leather.

"Oh, there you are!"

Avery and Natalie turned in unison to see a willowy girl with cascading auburn hair and a freckled complexion sweep across the marble floor. She wore a fluttery white Milly sundress and enormous D&G sunglasses perched on her head. She looked as though she'd just stepped off her private yacht. "I was coming about that Givenchy. So sorry I didn't get your messages—I was in Sagaponack. My cell phone service is awful out there." She sighed deeply, as if a weak cell phone signal in the Hamptons were the greatest tragedy she'd ever encountered.

"Thanks again for holding it." The girl grabbed the satchel from Avery's hands, as if Avery's job was to hold it for her. What the fuck?

"Jack Celine." Natalie turned to the girl with a tight smile. "Unfortunately, because we do have a release policy and we have someone interested, I'm afraid that we'll have to put you back on the waiting list." She concluded with a brisk nod, and Avery detected a note of pride in her voice.

Avery smiled a too bad smile at the girl, feeling giddy. No one could possibly have this bag at Constance. It seemed all the more valuable now that she saw how much it was in demand. Avery reached for the purse, but the girl made no effort to loosen her grip on the brown leather handle.

"I can see why you need a new bag." Jack glanced pointedly

at Avery's worn Louis Vuitton speedy purse. It had been her thirteenth-birthday present from her grandmother, and it was well loved, as she would have put it. "There are some outside you might be interested in," she finished.

Avery narrowed her blue eyes at the girl and gripped the cognac bag's shoulder strap. Outside? As in, the tacky knockoffs on the street? She was speechless.

"Now that that's settled," Jack went on, tightening her grasp around the Givenchy's handle, "can we please take care of this?" she asked haughtily, her green eyes flashing.

Natalie drew herself up to her full height of five foot two. She stood comically between the two girls, who faced each other eye to eye five inches above her head. "That's the only one we have," she began authoritatively. "It's a limited edition and rather fragile, so I'm sure you both will be able to work something out." She reached for their fingers, trying to pry them from the bag's leather handles.

"I don't think that will be necessary," Avery said, giving the purse a sharp tug that surprised Jack. She stumbled forward, losing her grip. Take that, bitch, Avery smirked.

Before Jack could regain her balance, Avery strode quickly away across the marble floor of Barneys, clutching the satchel protectively against her chest, like a football player headed for the end zone. Avery had gotten here first, and she was going to leave here first, with the bag that was rightfully hers. Only ten yards separated her from the cashier.

Avery couldn't help herself and turned around to glare at Jack victoriously. It was the Carlyle equivalent of a touchdown dance. The girl's face had drained of its perfect tan, and her green eyes looked more confused than angry. Avery grinned, feeling giddy.

But all of a sudden, a hideous buzzing sound erupted around her. She looked around in annoyance but couldn't see where the buzzing was coming from. Not daring to hesitate, she continued to walk, feeling a surge of victory.

"Excuse me, miss?" A burly security guard appeared in front of her. His name tag read Knowledge, and he looked like he stopped Upper East Side schoolgirls all the time.

Avery looked up in confusion. She tried to sidestep him, but he moved his bulk in front of her with ease.

She's not the first girl to make a run for it in Barneys!

"Give me the bag, baby girl, and it'll all be over," Knowledge said gently and quietly, holding on to Avery's thin arm. She could feel his gold-ringed fingers making an indentation on her tan skin.

And then, her blues eyes widening in shock, Avery realized they thought she was trying to steal the bag.

"I was going to pay for it," she said, trying not to sound desperate. She wordlessly handed him the bag. Shit, shit, shit.

Natalie joined them, whisking the satchel out of Knowledge's hands. Avery felt red splotches begin to form on her chest and face, which always happened when she was upset.

"I really think they should have an age limit for some floors, don't you?" Avery overheard one white-haired lady say loudly to her female friend with overly teased red hair wearing a leopard print Norma Kamali shirtdress. Avery suddenly felt like she was about five years old.

"I was going to pay for it," she repeated loudly. "The checkout counter wasn't well marked." Even as she said it, she cringed. Checkout counter? She sounded like she had taken a wrong turn at Target.

She shook her head, trying to appear supremely irritated and reached into her own LV-monogrammed purse. She would pull her brand-new black AmEx out of her red-and-green-striped Gucci wallet. Then everyone would see it was all an unfortunate mistake and apologize and give her loads of complimentary products for the inconvenience.

"Luckily, the exit is well marked," Natalie replied icily. She was enjoying this, Avery realized. She lowered her voice. "Don't worry. We're not going to call your parents." And with that, she whirled around on her black Prada pumps and walked back to Jack, who was waiting with a steely smirk on her irritatingly freckled face.

"I just had to have it for the first day of school," Jack said dramatically. She took the purse in her hands, examining it as if to make sure Avery hadn't dirtied it with her sticky fingers.

"Your shopping trip is over, honey." Knowledge's soft voice interrupted her awful reverie as two more security guards escorted her out a side entrance on Sixty-first Street.

The door closed with a thud.

Avery's faced burned. She half expected an angry Barneys mob to follow her as she scurried away, but instead two thirtysomething women pushed their Bugaboo strollers past her, chatting about the best nursery schools. White-gloved doormen stood outside rows of luxury apartment buildings. A red double-decker bus headed uptown toward Central Park. Avery felt her heart slow down. No one had a clue who she was, or what had just happened. She readjusted her headscarf and crossed the street with her chin held high. This wasn't Nantucket, where everything was broadcast until infinity. This was New York, a city of over eight million people, where Avery could do whatever—be whoever—she wanted to be. So what if she didn't get the Givenchy satchel? She still had the new patent leather Miu Miu maryjanes she'd bought yesterday and her lucky pearls from Grandmother Avery. She was sure she could even go back to Barneys tomorrow and no one would recognize her.

As she crossed the avenue, a cute guy in a gray Riverside Prep T-shirt and Yankees cap jogged by, smiling at her. She smiled broadly back, batting her carefully mascaraed eyes. That spoiled bitch from hell could have the bag. Tomorrow, Avery Carlyle would begin her brand-new life at her brand-new school and Jack Celine would be a distant memory—some jerk who stole her purse, never to be heard from again.

Don't be so sure. New York may be a huge city, but it's one small town. . . .

Read the rest of

gossip girl
the carlyles

Available everywhere May 2008

Q&A with Cecily von Ziegesar

First job: Waitress at restaurant with roaches.

Worst job: Waitress at restaurant with roaches.

Favorite place: Primrose Hill in London.

Favorite NYC hotspot: My patio, where I planted all these flowering trees and bamboo. I like to have friends over and hang out back there until the mosquitoes drive us indoors.

Guilty pleasure: *American Idol.*

Best friend's first name: Pony Boy (my nearly hairless cat).

Good luck charm: Diamond earrings.

When you were a little girl, you thought you would grow up to be a...? Writer, always. I wanted to be a ballet dancer too, and a horse back rider, but writing won out in the end.

All-time favorite American Idol: Kelly. I'm a huge fan.

Favorite designer: I don't just have one favorite designer. I have more like twenty. I like Diane von Furstenberg and Marc Jacobs and Theory and Issa and Celine. But I buy a lot of clothes at Target. I just bought this amazing little black dress there by Patrick Robinson, one of those visiting designers that did a line just for Target. It fits so perfectly and it was only $27.99.

Favorite jeans: My favorite jeans are Joes Jeans and Imitation of Christ.

Favorite movie: *It's a Wonderful Life* (I cry every time).

Biggest fashion blunder: White duck feather jacket.

Next vacation destination: I'm going to Rio de Janeiro soon with my husband. I'm very excited—I've always wanted to go to Brazil! You won't catch me in one of those string thong bikini things though. Hello?!

French fry dip: Stupid question: ketchup.

Astrological sign: Cancer.

Lucky color: Don't have one. I'm fickle that way.

Midnight snack: Sleep.

Celebrity crush: Madonna (she takes herself so seriously!).

Favorite book: *The Great Gatsby.*

Item you can't live without: Fresh air? Not really, I'm very low maintainance. But I like my watered-down grapefruit juice first thing in the morning, followed by two cups of very strong milky coffee.

poppy